BROCK

A CHRISTIAN ROMANTIC SUSPENSE

OATH OF HONOR
BOOK 2

LAURA SCOTT

CHAPTER ONE

Police officer Brock Greer stood on the rocky shoreline overlooking Lake Michigan, ignoring the cold March wind blasting his face while trying to shake off his despair. He shouldn't have canceled the appointment with his lawyer. He should just file the divorce paperwork and be done with it.

It was some sort of weakness inside of him that prevented him from taking that final step to end a marriage that had barely begun. He hadn't seen Liana since she'd left him four months ago, after their fight when he'd caught a glimpse of her text message with a guy named Troy agreeing to meet up the following day.

He'd accused her of cheating. She'd asked why he didn't trust her, then she had turned and walked out of their condo. The morning after their heated exchange, she'd simply texted a brief message. *This won't work. I'm sorry.*

And that was that.

For long minutes, he was numb to the icy blast washing over him. It matched the coldness in his heart. But he finally turned, hunched his shoulders, and walked toward the city.

It wasn't smart to come back to the places he and Liana had been together. Living in their Third Ward condo was hard enough.

The condo was too far away to walk from here. He'd have to grab a rideshare. His stomach rumbled with hunger, he'd skipped lunch again, so he forced himself to head to the closest restaurant to grab something to eat.

His feet took him straight to Lu Chen's, a Chinese restaurant that had been one of Liana's favorites. He almost turned away to find someplace else but then stubbornly opened the door and stepped inside.

He liked Lu Chen's food; they had a wide selection of authentic meals to choose from. He stood in the doorway, looking around the place to make sure Liana wasn't there. He didn't really expect to see her seated in the small dining room. He'd come there often those first few weeks after she'd left him but hadn't found her.

Tonight was no different. Although he was keenly aware of several customers openly staring at him. It took a moment to realize he was still wearing his uniform. The suspicion in their dark gazes made him sigh.

Whatever. He knew some people disliked cops on sight. There wasn't anything he could do about that, though. He wouldn't be here long enough for his career to be a problem. He ordered his favorite meal as a takeout, then wove his way through the restaurant toward the restrooms. He stopped abruptly when he heard low voices speaking in rapid-fire Chinese.

Too fast for him to understand; besides, he was rusty from lack of practice over these past few months. Liana had taught him the basics, but what he heard now sounded like gibberish.

He couldn't explain why he'd pushed open the

swinging door to the kitchen. Maybe it was the female voice that lured him in. He frowned and stepped in farther.

"Get out!" The words in furious English were aimed at him. His eyes widened when he saw a tall Asian man and a beautiful mixed-race Asian woman. She looked just like Liana.

She was Liana!

"No police!" The tall Asian abruptly grabbed Liana and pressed a gun to her temple. Brock's jaw dropped as Liana stared at him with annoyance. "Get out! Now!"

"Okay, remain calm, there's no reason to panic." He lifted his hands, palms forward, to show he wasn't a threat, even as icy fingers of fear ran down his back. What was going on? Why was Liana here? And why was this man threatening to kill her?

"I'm warning you." The Asian man's gaze bored into his as he spoke in a low, threatening tone. "You will turn and leave now. Or she is dead."

"I'm leaving." His hostage negotiation skills were failing him, big time. Brock prided himself on talking people down from the ledge, but this guy was intently focused on the mission at hand. And he had the distinct feeling the Asian would kill Liana without a second thought. He took a half step backward, forcing a calm serenity into his voice that he was far from feeling. "There's no reason to hurt her. This is all a big misunderstanding. I only came for dinner, nothing more."

The Asian scowled and pressed the gun more firmly against Liana's temple, using enough force to make her wince. Brock took another step back. They were too far away for him to do anything but retreat. He noticed the kitchen staff darted a few quick glances in his direction but then returned to their work of chopping and cooking.

As if there wasn't anything unusual about seeing a man holding a gun at a woman's head, threatening to kill her.

"I don't know what's going on here. I took a wrong turn. I only wanted to use the restroom. I don't want any trouble." One more step backward and he'd be out of the kitchen space, and the door would swing shut. Brock hesitated, unwilling to simply leave Liana in his man's hands. Yet what choice did he have?

Liana spoke in Chinese, and this time, he caught part of what she was saying. *You're being stupid; he's not here because of us.*

Us? As in the tall Asian was Troy? The man she'd left him for?

Brock turned to his right so that he could subtly reach for his weapon. A blur of movement caught the corner of his eye. Yanking his gun free of the holster, he dropped to one knee and brought the weapon around. Liana must have caught the Asian off guard, because she'd twisted out of his grasp and held the gun she'd taken from him.

"Go!" She almost spat the word at Brock. "Leave us!"

Leave them? Not happening. Brock didn't understand what was going on here, but he wasn't leaving her with a man who'd threatened to kill her. Instead, he rushed forward, taking the guy's other arm and wrenching it behind his back.

Drawing handcuffs from his utility belt, he proceeded to slap the silver bracelets onto the Asian man's wrists. Liana heaved a sigh and stepped back and tossed the Asian man's weapon onto the closest surface.

"Why are you here?" Her voice was a low hiss as she raked her free hand through her long, straight black hair. "Do you realize what you've done?"

"I came to get dinner." He finished cuffing the man,

then turned to look at her. "And yeah, looks like I may have saved your life."

"Not even close!" She took a step toward him, her dark eyes flashing with anger. "You blew my cover."

Her cover? He shook his head as if unable to comprehend what she was saying. "What cover? What are you talking about?"

She sighed and tipped her head back to stare at the ceiling as if seeking wisdom in the face of his stupidity. And in that moment, he understood.

Liana had been working as an undercover police officer.

DESPITE HER ANNOYANCE at how Brock had burst into the kitchen, sending Bai Chow into panic mode and ultimately blowing her cover, Liana had to admit it was good to see him. She'd missed him terribly.

More than she'd thought possible. But not enough to distract her from the mission.

The way he stared at her in complete shock made her realize he hadn't known anything about the op. And if that was true, why was he here?

"You're working undercover?" Brock's tone was incredulous. "All this time? Ever since you left?"

"Yes." She swallowed a sigh, knowing her handler would not be happy about this latest turn of events. Months of work were about to be flushed down the drain.

"Get him out of here." She waved at Bai. "Book him for menacing with a deadly weapon. I have to go."

"Where?" Brock shoved Bai aside and took a step toward her. "Don't you think you owe me an explanation?"

"Not really." She did, of course, but not here. And not now. "Later, okay? We'll meet at PK's."

He shook his head, taking another step forward. "Nope. Don't trust you'll show. In fact, I'd bet my pension that you won't."

His comment hurt, although she understood why he was leery. Leaving him hadn't been easy. But it had been a necessity. She held his gaze, willing him to believe her. "I promise I'll be at PK's in one hour."

Brock reached for her arm, but she moved quickly to avoid his grasp. Then she turned and fled through the kitchen, heading for the back door. She felt certain he wouldn't follow, not when he had Bai Chow in custody.

Outside, the cold air made her shiver. Her mind whirled as she tried to come up with a mitigation strategy. The kitchen staff at Lu Chen's were well trained to ignore anything that happened on the premises. As far as she could tell, they hadn't paid her and Bai's altercation any attention. Not even when he'd pulled a gun on her. Yet the Chinese people in general were wary of the police. It would not go over well that a cop had entered the kitchen, taking their restaurant manager into custody.

Think. She needed to think! She couldn't lose the ground she'd gained over the past few months.

Bringing her one step closer to the man only known as Twisted Snake, the leader of the sex-trafficking operation.

And to saving Mai Shi's life.

Darting through streets and back alleys, Liana tried to come up with a plausible excuse. One that would protect her cover. She could try to turn the tables on Bai. Make it sound as if he'd led the police to the restaurant. She had been there first, with Bai arriving fifteen minutes later.

She nodded to herself as she walked swiftly through the street. Yes, she may be able to make the scenario work.

Unless Bai Chow decided to talk. She inwardly winced. If that happened? There would be no way to salvage the operation.

When she'd put at least a mile between herself and the restaurant, she pulled out her disposable phone. She slowed her pace and did her best to calm her breathing. After a long moment, she made the call.

"Bai was followed to Lu," she said, using the abbreviated version of the restaurant's name. "The police arrived."

The curse on the other end of the phone was slightly reassuring. So far, so good.

"Of course, he was frisked, and his weapon confiscated. He was arrested on the spot," she continued. "I managed to slip out the back."

"Stay out of sight," the male voice instructed her. "I will be in touch."

"Soon, I hope," she agreed, then quickly disconnected from the call. If she pressed too much, it would look suspicious.

Even now, she couldn't be sure Muchin had believed her version of events. She swallowed hard and shook her head. What had possessed Brock to show up at the restaurant? To come into the kitchen of all things?

She abruptly stopped. Had he been following her?

No, she always made sure there was no one behind her. And she felt certain Brock's surprise at seeing her had been real.

Rotten timing, she thought with a sigh. Or maybe divine intervention.

Working undercover meant she couldn't follow any of her old routines in her previous life. Most of the time, she didn't even think about her real identity. She'd become Feng Chi in her mind. Not Liana Wong.

But seeing Brock had brought memories of their time together cascading over her like warm waves washing over the shore. Reminding her of the wonderful life she'd turned her back on.

The love they'd shared. Well, at least on her part. Brock hadn't loved her the way she had loved him.

She turned a corner and nearly ran into a large African American man. Murmuring an apology in Chinese, she attempted to skirt around him.

A beefy hand shot out and grabbed her arm. She whirled and lashed out with her foot, kicking him in the groin. He instantly released her, letting out a howl of pain.

As he doubled over, cursing at her, Liana broke into a run, putting badly needed distance between them. She was annoyed with herself for letting her guard down. This area of the city that had become her home turf wasn't exactly a nice part of town.

She needed to keep her wits about her. No more thinking about Brock until she made it to PK's.

Liana turned down her street, keeping a sharp eye out for anyone lingering nearby. She needed to get her vehicle, a rusty sedan that looked to be on its last leg but had a decent engine, thanks to the undercover squad at the MPD. And she also needed to grab her weapon. Normally, she didn't carry one, as that wasn't part of her role. Yet she couldn't be sure Muchin would believe her story. If he didn't and decided to send someone after her, she needed to be ready.

She really, really wished Brock hadn't blown her cover.

Slipping into her apartment building, she took the stairs to the second floor. She paused outside her door, listening intently before putting her key in the lock and pushing the door open.

Standing off to the side, she peered quickly around the doorjamb to scan the room. Nothing seemed out of place. She always took care to scatter items around in what appeared to be haphazard way.

But she knew exactly where every item was supposed to be.

Reassured her apartment hadn't been searched, she ducked inside and closed the door behind her. Then she cautiously crept toward the hallway where the bedroom and bathroom were located.

Both were empty.

There was no time to waste. She entered her bedroom and quickly used a screwdriver to open a panel in her window air conditioner to retrieve her service weapon. Not the most original hiding spot in the world, but the stark apartment didn't offer many options.

Then she grabbed her keys from beneath a pile of mail and headed back outside. This part of the city didn't have luxuries like underground parking lots. Or any parking lots. There was only street parking that was on a first come, first served basis. And in winter, the rule of parking on only one side of the street, alternating days to make room for snowplows, made those precious parking spaces even more difficult to find.

Her vehicle was four blocks away, but she didn't go straight there. Taking her usual surveillance precautions, she headed in the opposite direction for three blocks before circling back, her sharp gaze making sure she hadn't been followed.

By the time she reached her sedan, her fingers were numb from the cold. She only wore thin gloves and a worn coat in keeping with her disguise of living in a low-income neighborhood and had to blow into her cupped palms to warm up before she could get inside the vehicle.

All this because Brock had stumbled into her meeting with Bai.

Rather than scraping the ice from her windshield, she sat in the car and waited for it to melt. Then she had to finagle the car back and forth to get out of the tight space, before heading to the Third Ward.

Patty's Kitchen was a small diner not far from the condo she'd once shared with Brock. They had enjoyed many pancake breakfasts there, and the occasional lunch too. They hadn't gone there for dinner often, but she knew they'd be open until nine. Just pulling into the small parking lot filled her with nostalgia.

She hadn't allowed herself to think about her life with Brock. The only way to survive an undercover assignment like this was to immerse yourself in the role. As if she wasn't Brock's wife and fellow cop.

She was Feng Chi, a woman involved in Muchin's sex-trafficking operation. Of course, her girls were not given to prostitution rings the way Muchin paid her to do. She managed to help them escape but provided the cash to Muchin through Bai Chow as if they were on the job.

Constantly walking a fine line between saving girls and being caught and killed.

But now she sat in her car, staring at the restaurant, desperately wishing she could just walk back into Brock's arms, leaving the horrifying world of sex trafficking behind. Especially since she hadn't been able to find Mai Shi.

It was tempting to put the gear shift into reverse and drive far away from there. But she couldn't do that to Brock.

Not again. Leaving him the first time had been difficult

enough.

Drawing in a deep breath, she shut down the car and slid out from behind the wheel. She headed inside, easily spotting Brock in the corner booth.

Their booth.

His green gaze pierced hers as she moved forward. His expression remained hard as stone, without an ounce of welcome or compassion.

His frank hostility caught her off guard.

"I guess I should be honored you kept your word for once," he said as she slid across from him.

She shrugged. "I told you I would."

"You said a lot of things, Liana," he shot back. "Like 'until death do us part.'"

It was no surprise he'd tossed their wedding vows in her face. She'd known she'd hurt him, but she also wasn't going to sit there like a lamb, tolerating his verbal punching. She held his gaze. "Be civil or I'm gone."

Brock's gaze narrowed. He opened his mouth, then seemed to think better of it. A server came over with menus. "Can I get you anything to drink?"

"Coffee," she and Brock answered in unison.

The woman laughed. "I'll be right back."

There was a long silence before Brock spoke. "Who is Troy?"

She nodded, remembering their argument. She waited until their server brought their coffee before saying, "Lieutenant Troy Wallace. He's my handler in this undercover op."

"Are you sleeping with him?" Brock asked.

Her fingers itched to slap his face. "No, Brock. I'm working an undercover assignment. One I was forbidden to tell you about."

"That's insane. Why wouldn't you tell me about it?"

"Because you would have interfered. And don't try to pretend otherwise."

He scowled but didn't argue. He knew she was right.

"You saw my text messages because you went through my phone." She kept her voice even. "I assume you didn't trust me back then either, so it's no surprise you don't trust me now. That's your choice, Brock. I wouldn't have played up having a relationship with Troy if you hadn't jumped to that conclusion."

He scoffed. "You really expect me to believe that?"

"Not really." She shrugged, battling a sudden wave of exhaustion. "You're the only one who can decide what you believe. I can't force you or change your mind." She paused, then asked, "What happened to Bai Chow?"

"I asked my teammate Raelyn to book him on menacing with a deadly weapon." He played with a napkin, shredding it into small pieces. It was something Brock did when he was emotionally distraught. Not that he'd ever admit to such a thing. "Is Chow part of your undercover assignment?"

"Yes." She leaned forward. "What were you doing there, Brock? What made you come into the kitchen of Lu Chen in your uniform?"

He pushed the pile of shredded napkin aside. "I have no idea why I went inside. I ordered takeout and was going to use the bathroom. Hearing your low voices, I pushed the door to the kitchen open." He shook his head. "I was shocked to see you there."

She believed him, unlike the way he hadn't believed her. "Yeah, I was surprised to see you too. I can only hope you didn't completely blow my cover. I did my best to put the blame for your arrival on Bai Chow."

His gaze narrowed. "You're not seriously sticking with the assignment?"

When they'd first started dating, she'd been touched by the way he'd seemed so protective of her. Now it was downright annoying. "Yes, I am. So I need you to promise not to tell anyone about seeing me. Or what I'm doing." She frowned. "I hope you didn't tell Raelyn."

"I didn't, but I don't think it's smart of you to keep playing whatever role Troy has assigned. One hour ago, Bai was about to kill you."

"Because he thought I brought the police into the kitchen." She suddenly realized that agreeing to meet with Brock was a mistake. "Look, I came here as promised. Now it's your turn to uphold your end of the deal. Do not tell anyone within the tactical team about what I'm doing or go to Troy with this." She hesitated, then added, "Unless you hate me so much you want to see killed."

"Why are you doing this?" There was a hint of desperation in his voice. "There's no reason for you to put your life on the line."

For my mother. She didn't say the words, though, knowing he wouldn't understand. She rose to her feet. "I have to go. Thanks for the coffee."

"Liana, wait!"

She ignored him. Heading outside, the March wind kicked up, snatching the door from her fingers. After wrestling it closed, she turned to head toward her car. A nearby car was running. Then the window slowly rolled down.

Gun!

Liana hit the ground, rolling toward her sedan while pulling her weapon as gunfire shattered the silence of the night.

CHAPTER TWO

Brock was already halfway through the restaurant heading to the door when he saw the gun aimed at Liana. He rushed forward as Liana hit the ground, rolling toward her sedan. He pulled his weapon and slammed the door open. He fired toward the car, but it was already driving away.

Without regard for his own safety, Brock ran into the cold, chasing after the vehicle on foot. It was an older model sedan. He put on a burst of speed to get close enough to get the license plate, but there wasn't one.

The passenger window opened again, and a man's head wearing a ski mask emerged. Expecting the gun, Brock stopped his pursuit, diving toward the side of the road, well out of the gunman's range.

Breathing hard, he watched as the car disappeared around a corner. He hung his head for a moment, wishing he'd been faster. Then a horrible thought hit, and he jumped to his feet and ran back to Patty's Kitchen.

Would Liana be there? Or had she disappeared in the time it took for him to chase the shooter?

His heart was lodged in his throat as he covered the

distance. Then he slowly relaxed when he saw Liana on her phone, standing near her car. The window and side door had been peppered by bullets. It gave him hope they'd find slugs embedded inside.

"Thanks, Troy." Liana lowered her phone. "Did you get the plate number?"

He shook his head. "There wasn't one. Just a crumpled paper taped to the inside back window." It was common practice for these guys to use a sign designed to look like a temporary license plate when in reality the car was either stolen or not registered with the state.

She grimaced. "That figures."

He raked his gaze over her. "You're not hurt?"

"I'm fine." She sighed. "I guess this is solid proof my cover has been blown."

He should feel guilty over the inadvertent role he'd played in outing her but didn't. Not that he wanted any undercover operation to go sideways, but the idea of Liana being in the thick of danger made his skin crawl.

"We'll head back to the condo." He nodded toward his black SUV that was parked in the farthest corner of the small lot. "We can decide our next steps there."

"Our next steps?" She frowned. "This is my job, not yours."

"I'm a part of it now." For a moment, he wondered if God had sent him to Lu Chen's that evening. It was the only explanation he could come up with as to why he'd entered the kitchen. "Let's go, Liana. It's too cold to stand around here arguing."

She sighed, glancing back at her damaged sedan. "Fine, but I'll need to meet with Troy very soon."

Just hearing Troy's name put his teeth on edge. He

hated the guy without laying eyes on him. But he managed to swallow his protest and nod. "I understand."

A flicker of surprise widened her eyes, but she didn't respond, falling into step beside him. It had been months since he'd been this close to Liana, and it took all his willpower not to pull her into his arms.

He didn't have that privilege anymore. All because she'd left him to do an undercover job. What wife did that?

Using his key fob, he unlocked the SUV. Force of habit had him opening the passenger door for her. Once they were both settled, he cranked the heat. She was shivering but smiled when she pressed the button for her seat warmer.

"I missed seat warmers more than you can imagine," she murmured.

More than me? He bit back the sharp response. As much as he hated to admit it, he needed to swallow his pride and let go of his anger. The more important thing right now was that a gunman had found Liana at PK's. If not for her quick reflexes, she may have been injured or worse.

Dead. The very thought filled him with horror. During these past four months, he'd nursed his anger and resentment, but he always knew Liana was out there alive and well. Enjoying her time with Troy, or so he'd assumed.

That she'd left him to participate in a deep cover assignment had never crossed his mind.

The trip to their condo didn't take long. When he pulled into the underground parking garage, she glanced around the brightly lit space with a keen gaze.

There was an edge to Liana that hadn't been there before. She'd always been a phenomenal cop, but there was something more lethal about her now. It made him wonder if she'd faced similar situations to Bai Chow holding a gun to her head.

He swallowed hard, trying not to imagine the worst.

"Brock?" Liana's voice pulled him from his thoughts.

He turned to look at her. Then realized he was sitting in the parking space, not moving. "What?"

"Would you rather go someplace other than the condo?"

"No, this is fine." He shut down the SUV and opened his door. Liana followed suit, following him to the elevator. He'd purchased the third-floor condo overlooking the Milwaukee River five years ago. He owned it, which was why he'd stayed there after Liana had left him. And maybe partially because he'd hoped she would return at some point. When they stepped off the elevator, he pulled out his key and unlocked the door.

Liana brushed past him to step inside. She glanced around curiously, no doubt making note of the lack of change in the time she'd been gone.

Even her clothes were still in the closet.

"Do you want more coffee?" He didn't drink, and neither did Liana, but a stiff shot of whiskey would have been nice.

"Sure. I—uh, do you have anything to eat?" Her hesitant question had him turning to glance at her.

"I can make omelets," he offered. "Unfortunately, I never did get my Lu Chen's carryout order."

"An omelet sounds good." She hesitated, then offered, "I can make it if you like."

He shook his head as he continued to fill the coffeemaker with water. "I'll take care of it." Having Liana cook for them would be too much like old times. Not that he hadn't done his fair share of cooking and cleaning; they'd always pitched in together to do household chores. "How much of this undercover operation can you tell me?"

"Not much." She abruptly stood. "If you don't mind, I'd like to clean up."

"Sure thing. You—ah, know where everything is." Could this be any more awkward?

After Liana left the kitchen, he busied himself with making omelets. It helped to have something to do with his hands, but he found himself keenly listening for sound coming from their bedroom.

He gave himself a mental shake. Time to get a grip. Liana wasn't home for good. This was a temporary arrangement as they discussed their next steps on her case.

An undercover operation he was now a part of, whether she liked it or not. He was half tempted to contact Lieutenant Troy Wallace for himself but decided he should give Liana some time to come around to his way of thinking.

At least, he hoped she'd come around. He had the power of the tactical unit behind him should they need backup. That had to count for something.

He had two fry pans going with a large omelet cooking in each when Liana returned to the kitchen. She'd showered and changed into well-worn jeans and a sweater, looking more like the wife he remembered rather than the woman held at gunpoint by Bai Chow.

"Smells good." She moved past him to fill a cup with coffee.

It was a scene from their past. Preparing meals together in this kitchen. Only this time, there wasn't cuddling and sharing coffee from the same mug.

He needed to stop tripping down memory lane. He couldn't ignore the past four months she'd been gone. Doing who knew what within some horrible criminal organization.

After he slid one omelet, then the other onto two plates, he turned from the stove. Liana had taken her usual chair, leaving him to drop into the one next to her.

She lowered her coffee and smiled. "Thanks, Brock."

"You're welcome." He thought about how Rhy, Joe, and even Steele would have said grace. He'd resisted the urge to formally join their church, but this moment seemed to call for a blessing. Liana was alive, despite being held at gunpoint and then being used for target practice. He found himself silently praying for God to continue keeping her safe.

They ate in silence for a moment. After four months of not having her here, he wasn't sure where to start.

"I'll need to call Troy again later," she said, interrupting his thoughts. "He's trying to get a line on who Bai may have spoken too."

He frowned. "There wouldn't have been enough time for Bai to have spoken to anyone about what went down at Lu Chen's. Don't you think it's more likely that one of the kitchen staff got the word out?"

She looked thoughtful. "Maybe, although Bai pays them well to ignore the business side of things."

"And the business side of things often involves using a gun?" He struggled to remain calm. Had she known the place was a front for criminal activity all along?

She shrugged. "Sometimes. And how would any of the kitchen staff know what PK's is? I purposefully didn't use the actual name of the diner."

"Who did you talk to after leaving Lu Chen's?" He tried not to show how much he hated the idea of her working undercover. It was a lost cause anyway; the damage had already been done.

"My crime boss, but only for a minute. I told him that Bai was arrested."

"Maybe your crime boss has a tracker on your phone." He liked that idea even less. "You shouldn't keep it with you. We'll need to head out soon so you can toss it somewhere."

"I tossed it beneath my vehicle at Patty's Kitchen, just to be safe." She pulled out a different disposable phone. "I only use this one to call Troy."

He really needed to lose the knee-jerk flash of anger every time she mentioned the guy's name. Being angry wouldn't help the situation. She'd claimed she wasn't sleeping with Troy, so he tried to let it go. To be honest, discovering she was working undercover all this time, rather than cheating on him, should have made him feel better.

Except it didn't. Mostly because he couldn't believe she'd just walked away. From them. From their marriage. For a job? That was another slap to the face.

"I'll need to buy a replacement phone for the one I left behind," Liana went on, as if oblivious to his turmoil. "I'll need to reconnect with Mu—er, my crime boss soon."

"Not tonight." He would have preferred they never leave the condo again, but that wasn't feasible. The thought of leaving for work in the morning had him straightening in his chair. While Liana was chatting with Troy, he'd call Joe and ask for a temporary leave of absence. Just for a few days, until he understood what Liana's plans were. Despite her plan to return to her undercover role, he highly doubted that would be possible now that Bai had been arrested.

And no matter how well paid the kitchen staff may be, he doubted they'd keep their mouths shut for long.

She frowned, then shrugged. "I guess it can wait until morning." She toyed with her fork for a moment, pushing a mushroom around on her plate, then asked, "Are we still married?"

He froze, remembering the three separate occasions he'd canceled his meeting with his divorce lawyer. "Yeah. Unless you did some court filing that I'm not aware of."

"No, there hasn't been time." She took another bite of her omelet. "I'm a little surprised to find out you didn't. Take legal action, I mean."

"I was going to." He spoke without thinking. Maybe it was time for some honesty. "I set up an appointment with a divorce lawyer, but since I wasn't sure where you were living, I kept putting it off. I, uh, tried to find you but couldn't." He didn't add that he'd assumed she'd moved in with Troy and had given up without digging too deep.

The last thing he'd wanted was to see her in the arms of another man.

"I was never with Troy the way you assumed," she said as if reading his thoughts. Or maybe she was just that good at reading his mood. "Like I said before, you can either trust me or not. Your choice." She ate the last bite of her omelet, then stood and carried her empty plate to the sink. "I'll need a few minutes of privacy. I hope you don't mind if I use the bedroom to make my call."

He told himself not to think about her being in their bedroom. "I don't mind."

"Thanks, Brock." She turned and retreated from the room. For long moments, he just sat there, trying to regain his equilibrium.

Then he pulled out his own phone to call Joe. After making the arrangements for a few days off, citing personal issues, he began washing dishes.

Tomorrow morning he'd follow Liana, hopefully without her noticing. Because even if their marriage couldn't be salvaged, he couldn't simply stand aside, letting her stroll into the lion's den without backup.

He was a part of this whether she liked it or not.

LIANA COULDN'T BELIEVE Brock hadn't changed the condo in the months she'd been gone. She'd expected to find her things boxed up and stored in the hallway closet. It was downright creepy to walk into the bedroom to shower and change as if she'd never left.

That he hadn't filed for divorce was another shock. The man she'd married would have closed the door on their past and moved on.

Or so she'd have thought.

No point in reading more into that than was warranted. She sat on the edge of the bed, staring at her phone. She really did want to call Troy, but that was partially an excuse for time away from Brock. He seemed more intense than usual.

Or maybe she'd just forgotten what it was like being with him.

She closed her eyes for a moment, doing her best to remain strong. She'd loved Brock. Had thought he'd loved her too. And maybe he had.

But he hadn't trusted her.

When Troy Wallace had approached her about this assignment, she'd almost refused, knowing it would take her away from Brock for a significant amount of time. But when he'd told her about the organization run by Twisted Snake, and that her mother had been forced into prostitution twenty-five years ago, she'd been shocked. Liana knew she'd been adopted but hadn't known the circumstances around her birth.

Then Troy had dropped the second bomb, that he suspected her cousin Mai Shi had been taken by the same traffickers. And that had been enough for her to agree without hesitation to take on this role. In this case, her ethnicity had worked in her favor. The sex-trafficking ring was run by a former member of the Triad, a well-known and lethal arm of the Chinese Mafia. Much bigger in China and in the other large cities like New York, LA, and Chicago.

Her job would be to work her way up in the organization until she could meet Twisted Snake, the elusive leader of the ring. The thought of bringing down the man who'd ultimately killed her mother, while hopefully finding her cousin, had given her a sense of purpose. More so than simply being another cop on the street.

Troy had insisted she couldn't tell Brock about the assignment, and that was the biggest obstacle in her taking the job. She'd struggled internally with what to do.

When Brock had accused her of cheating with Troy, she'd taken it as a sign. Trust was always an issue with Brock; his mother had abandoned him as a toddler, and his father had abused him. He'd grown up in the foster system, while Liana had been blessed with wonderful adoptive parents.

Yet Brock had claimed to love her. Wasn't trust a part of love?

The fact that he could so easily believe she'd toss their wedding vows out the window to sleep with another man was infuriating and insulting. She'd walked out the door and told Troy she was in.

And that was the last time she'd seen Brock, until tonight.

Steeling her resolve not to get lost in the past, she dialed Troy's number. He picked up on the third ring. "Feng?" He always used her undercover name. "Is something wrong?"

Everything, she thought, feeling weary. "No, but I wanted to remind you that I need another set of wheels. Preferably something like the last one, a car that looks beat up and useless but has a good engine."

"I'm on it," he agreed. "I had your sedan towed to the police garage for processing. Don't worry, your name isn't attached to the vehicle."

"I know." Troy had done a great job of layering her cover. So much so that Brock apparently hadn't been able to find her. "I'll also need someone to swing by my apartment, make sure there isn't anyone staked out there, waiting for me to return."

There was a long pause as he digested her request. "You really think Muchin is onto you?"

She honestly didn't know what to think. "I hope not, but we need to cover all bases, just in case." Brock's question about tracking her phone had stuck. "I thought I smoothed things over with him, but he could have tracked me via my phone."

"A disposable phone? Not likely," Troy said in a dismissive tone. "Although he could have had someone follow you."

"There's always a way to find people, you know that." She'd worked hard to make sure she wasn't followed, but nothing was foolproof. "Just send an officer to the apartment, okay? Claim there's an anonymous tip about a stalker hanging out there."

"I'll take care of it." He paused, then asked, "Where are you now?"

"Safe." She wasn't going to tell him she was with Brock.

"I have cash and know how to stay under the radar."

"Okay, that's fine. Tomorrow at ten, at the usual location," Troy said.

"I'll be there." She ended the call and stared up at the ceiling for a moment. If she were smart, she'd get out of there and find a cash-only motel. She knew where they were; several were used by the Johns who hooked up with Muchin's girls.

Just thinking about what happened to those girls made her sick to her stomach. The only thing that had kept her going was knowing that if they caught Twisted Snake, the operation would fall apart.

Was that worth ruining her marriage? No. Yes.

Maybe.

With a sigh, she rose to her feet. Leaving the bedroom, she paused in the hallway long enough to snag a pillow and blanket from the closet. That too hadn't been touched in the time she'd been gone.

It was like stepping into a time warp. As if the four months she'd been gone had never happened.

Then again, she wouldn't be sleeping on the sofa if that were true. Shying away from those thoughts, she crossed the living room and tossed the pillow and blanket onto the sofa.

Brock turned from the cupboard, his gaze going from her to the sofa and back again. "Everything all set?"

"Yep." She forced a cheerful note into her tone. "No need to worry. I'll be out of your hair tomorrow."

His brow furrowed, but he nodded. "Okay. I guess I'll say good night, then."

"Good night." She took a moment to shake the blanket out, then removed her gun and set it within reach before stretching out on the sofa. At five feet seven inches, she wasn't tall or short, so her feet just barely reached the other end of the furniture. She punched the pillow, then settled back and closed her eyes. Sleep would be nice, and something that had been in short supply over these past few months. One thing she hadn't been prepared for was that living the life of a criminal was far from restful.

She'd always had to be on alert, waiting for something to go wrong.

Maybe that was why she'd come here tonight, instinctively seeking a bit of peace and quiet at the condo. But she hadn't taken her feelings for Brock into account. She was hyperaware of him moving in the kitchen. Even with her eyes closed, she could see him standing there with a dish towel tossed over one shoulder.

She caught a whiff of his musky scent as he moved past her to head to the bedroom. Shocking to discover how much she wanted to reach out and grasp his hand to prevent him from leaving.

He shut the lights off on his way, leaving only the glow of the moonlight filtering in through the windows.

Coming here was probably a mistake. She had taken the easy way out of the situation at PK's without thinking through the ramifications. She turned on the sofa, punched the pillow again, and tried to relax.

Memories of her time with Brock came rushing at her like water released by a dam. Every loving, tender moment of their courtship, their marriage. And yes, even their arguments, mostly small skirmishes until the last one.

Taking several deep breaths, she used yoga techniques to clear her mind. Going backward in time was useless. All she—and Brock, too, for that matter—could do was move forward.

Liana wasn't foolish enough to think they could pick up the shards of their marriage and rebuild. But maybe they could at least have some sort of truce, working through the details of their separation and ultimate divorce in a civil manner.

But that couldn't happen until after she'd identified the man known only as Twisted Snake.

It bothered her to think her hard work would be for naught. There had to be a way to convince Muchin she wasn't the one who'd caused Bai's arrest.

How? She had no idea.

Somehow, she must have fallen asleep because she abruptly awoke to a noise. At first, she had no idea where she was until the familiar surroundings filtered into her brain.

Brock's condo. Had he made a noise?

After listening for a long moment, she swung her legs over the edge of the sofa, slid her feet into her shoes, and reached for her weapon. Her instincts were clamoring at her that something was wrong.

The door handle jiggled again.

Someone was trying to pick the lock to get inside!

Moving silently, she headed to the bedroom. Brock had left the door ajar, so she pushed into the room and rested her hand on his shoulder. He shot upright in a heartbeat.

"What?" he whispered.

"Someone's trying to get in." As soon as the words left her mouth, she heard the sound of a door opening.

Brock rolled out of the bed, grabbed his service weapon from the nightstand, and stepped in front of her. And this was why Troy had insisted she couldn't tell Brock about her undercover assignment. Brock was constantly trying to protect her as if she wasn't a trained cop.

The condo wasn't that big, so she gestured for Brock to stand on one side of the bedroom door while she took the other. Less than a minute later, she heard the faintest brush of the intruder's clothing against the wall.

She'd anticipated the gunfire, but the sound was muted, as if the assailant was using a silencer.

In unison, she and Brock returned fire as she prayed none of the gunman's slugs would go through the wall, striking them.

CHAPTER THREE

The sound of return gunfire was deafening, but Brock still heard the thud as the assailant went down. His heart pounded in his chest as he acknowledged how close he and Liana had come to being killed in their own home.

His gaze met Liana's, and by mutual agreement, they held their fire for a long moment, listening intently. Then he quickly peeked around the doorjamb to check the hallway.

A man was lying on his back, his weapon on the floor beside him. Brock darted forward to grab the gun. Liana followed, kneeling beside the intruder to check for a pulse.

"He's gone." She reached up and removed his face mask. Brock had expected the assailant to be Asian, but he was a white male who didn't look the least bit familiar to him.

"Who is he?" he asked.

"I don't know." Liana patted the dead man's pockets. She pulled out a cheap disposable phone and a wad of cash. "No ID."

He hadn't really expected her to find one. He'd thought she may have recognized the guy from her undercover op. With a scowl, he wondered how this man had found them. "We need to get out of here."

"Yes, I'm sure Lettie and Albert from next door have already called the police." Liana scowled. "We need to hurry."

He turned away from the dead man. After taking a minute to put his shoes on and grab an MPD sweatshirt, he threaded his gun holster through his belt and stuffed extra ammo into his pockets.

While he did that, Liana tossed some items into a duffel bag. It struck him that they were working together as a team, reading each other's minds the way they once had.

As if she hadn't left him for an extremely dangerous undercover op.

Together, they moved through the dark condo to the door. He was irritated to realize the gunman had breached the condo so easily.

Rather than heading toward the elevator, Liana turned and pushed on the door leading to the stairwell. He followed her down to the main level, wondering how this had happened. Had the shooter at the diner noticed his SUV? If the gunman hadn't tracked his car here, then how were they found?

"Rideshare?" As if reading his mind, Liana glanced at him over her shoulder as they hit the landing.

"Yeah." Although it was the middle of the night, and he had no idea where to go, they needed a place to stay where they could stay off the radar. Maybe the American Lodge? It was way out in Brookland, but at least he knew the owner. "We need to get far away from this area of the city."

She frowned, then shrugged. "For now."

For now? Was she really going to try to salvage the op after they'd nearly been shot in their condo? The only reason they were alive at all was because Liana had been sleeping on the sofa.

Gritting his teeth to avoid an argument, they headed out the back door of the condo, knowing the police response to gunfire would likely be at the main entrance to the building. By tacit agreement, they walked several blocks away from the crime scene. There was a bar on the next corner, and at two in the morning, there were people milling around.

"This works." Liana gave a nod of approval. "Lots of rideshare drivers will be in the area."

"Yeah, thank goodness for bar time." He called for a ride and could see by the app that they were the third in line. He drew Liana toward the side of the building, scanning the area. "Do you think the gunman had backup nearby?"

"Good question." She was on high alert too. He had to remind himself that she was just as well trained as he was, despite her lithe frame. She frowned. "He either had a ride stashed nearby, or there's someone waiting for him to return."

"No car keys," he reminded her. "So likely someone waiting for him."

Her brow furrowed. "You're right. Let's hope they chose a place more remote than a packed bar. We should be safe around other people."

He silently agreed with her assessment. A full five minutes passed before their rideshare driver pulled up. Brock bent to look at the driver, making sure his face matched that on the app, then opened the door for Liana.

"You're headed for the American Lodge?" the driver asked once they were seated.

"Yes, thanks." He buckled his seatbelt. Liana arched a

brow but didn't argue. He belatedly realized he should have included her in the decision-making. "I know the owner, Gary Campbell," he said in a low voice. "He'll take cash with no questions asked."

"I see." She held his gaze in the darkness. "But Brookland is far away from where I need to be."

He bit his tongue to stop from saying something he'd regret. "We'll figure out our next steps in the morning."

"Yes, we will." She finally turned away, staring out the window. Thankfully, the trip to Brookland didn't take long at this hour of the night. There was little to no traffic on the interstate. As the rideshare driver navigated through the subdivision to where the American Lodge was located, Brock thought about his boss, Captain Rhy Finnegan. He lived in Brookland with his wife, Devon, and their five-month-old daughter, Colleen. He decided to reach out to Joe and Rhy the next morning. He could tell they would need backup for this.

Liana had called Troy. A few hours later, a gunman showed up at the condo. Maybe it was his irrational dislike of the guy, but that coincidence was impossible to ignore.

"Here you go." Their driver pulled up in front of the America Lodge lobby door.

"Thank you." Brock used the app to tip the driver, then slid out of the back seat. Liana followed, looking around curiously. He was glad to see all the window repairs had been completed.

There was a young kid behind the desk. "Can I help you?"

Brock showed the kid his badge. "I work for Rhy Finnegan and Joe Kingsley on the tactical team. We need a room and to pay in cash."

"Understood." The kid took the cash, then slid two room keys across the desk. "In the morning, I'll let Gary know you're here."

"Thanks." He turned and led the way back outside. The Finnegans had a long-standing relationship with Gary Campbell, hence the recent repairs to his windows. It was just two months ago that Steele's fiancée, Harper, had been hiding from gunmen only to be found here.

The team had come together to pay for the repairs, as the damage wasn't Gary's fault. Brock hoped the American Lodge was far off the radar of whoever had hired the gunman to come after them.

"That was slick," Liana said as he paused in front of room twelve, the last room on the ground level. "Nice to know this place is an option."

"Yeah," he agreed. "Gary Campbell is a former firefighter who was injured on the job. He offers discounts to cops and firefighters, which is nice." He set the duffel on one of the two beds. "He also has security cameras, which is an added benefit."

"But he's not monitoring them live, so they're only helpful after the fact." Liana ran her fingers through her hair. "Not complaining, just stating a fact."

"True." He eyed her warily. "We need to talk about how the gunman found us at the condo."

She frowned and took a seat on the edge of the second bed, closest to the bathroom. "There are only two real possibilities. Well, maybe three."

He sat across from her. "Let's hear them."

"The gunman showed up at Patty's Kitchen because one of the kitchen staff talked. That same gunman somehow figured out which SUV was yours and tracked it to the condo. Or the gunman recognized you and just showed up at the condo, hoping I'd be there." She met his gaze. "The last scenario is that my phone call to Troy was traced, leading the gunman to your condo."

The last scenario was the only one that made sense to him. "Even if the SUV had been tracked, there's no way a gunman would know which condo to break in to."

"Maybe, maybe not." She sighed. "I don't think we can afford to make any assumptions. If my cover is blown, and my real name is out there, it would be relatively easy to discover we're still married."

"You really don't think Troy is the leak?"

"No. Why would he leak my name now? This all started when you showed up at Lu Chen's in your cop uniform. That spooked Bai Chow, and from there, it's spiraled out of control."

He forced himself to think logically, without his emotional baggage clouding his judgment. She had a point. Why would Troy send gunmen after her now?

Yet a gunman had shown up at PK's. Then again at the condo.

"Okay." He scrubbed his hands over his face. "So now that we don't have my SUV, we should be safe."

"In theory." She grimaced. "I'm sorry, Brock. I didn't expect anyone to break in to the condo."

Sorry for the break-in? Not for leaving him? He forced himself to concentrate on the issue at hand. "We need to get some sleep. We'll need a game plan come morning."

She nodded and stood. "I'm calling first dibs. Give me a few minutes, then the bathroom is yours."

Her first dibs comment was like a punch to the gut. A casual phrase they'd said to each other hundreds of times during their short marriage. It was almost as if the four months they'd been apart hadn't happened.

He wanted to know everything about her undercover assignment. Yet he sensed she wasn't going to tell him much. Deep down, anger burned at how easily she'd walked away. Yet he also wanted nothing more than to pull her into his arms and kiss her.

It was difficult to know where things stood between them. He couldn't forget how she'd prioritized her career and this undercover operation over their marriage.

For all he knew, she wasn't interested in getting back together. She'd pretty much assumed he'd begun divorce proceedings.

Her comment at PK's echoed through his mind. *Be civil or I walk.*

He felt as if he was traversing a tightrope, digging into her case while doing his best not to make her angry for fear she'd leave without a second thought, heading right back into danger.

He desperately wanted, *needed* to keep her safe.

"All yours," Liana said, emerging from the bathroom.

He nodded. He rose and brushed past her. Yeah, there was no doubt about it. Being this close to Liana was killing him.

LIANA CAREFULLY SET her gun on the bedside table, then kicked off her shoes and crawled into bed. To her shame, she pretended to be asleep when Brock came out of the bathroom ten minutes later.

Coward, she silently rebuked. Yet she didn't move, concentrating instead on taking slow, deep breaths. Brock would want details about her undercover op. Troy had given her strict orders not to tell him, but now that her cover was blown, it probably didn't matter.

Unless there was a way to salvage this. How? She had no idea.

Months of hard work, playing a role to find the identity of Twisted Snake, would be all for naught if they couldn't figure out how to move forward. She couldn't let it go; she desperately needed to find and arrest the man who'd hurt her mother all those years ago.

And to find her teenage cousin Mai Shi.

Brock moved restlessly in his bed, no doubt struggling to put the recent shooting events aside the way she was.

She awoke several hours later, dawn brightening the horizon. Lifting her head, she glanced over to the other bed, but it was empty.

With a frown, she sat up, brushing her hair from her face. Then she heard running water in the bathroom.

This forced togetherness would be difficult to navigate. But since the gunman had broken into the condo listed in Brock's name, and likely had tagged his SUV somehow, he was elbow deep in this mess the same way she was.

She slid out of bed and reached for her weapon. After not wearing one every day during her assignment, it felt strange to strap it on now.

When Brock emerged, he looked surprised to see her up. "Hey."

"Good morning." She gestured to the bathroom. "Give me a few minutes, then we'll have coffee."

"Sounds good." He stepped aside so she could move past.

She quickly cleaned up, thinking this motel room wasn't

big enough for the two of them. Reuniting with Brock hadn't been a part of the plan.

Ten minutes later, they were sipping coffee at the minuscule table in the corner of the room. There was a long awkward silence before Brock asked, "Who is Troy's boss?"

She eyed him over the rim of her cup. "Captain Jorge Marbury. But we're not calling him."

"Liana." Brock leaned forward, resting his elbows on the table. "Your cover is blown, and there are gunmen trying to kill you."

"Thanks for pointing out the obvious," she drawled. "I'm aware of the danger, but I'm not ready to give up. I was thinking we should set up a meeting with Troy to discuss how we might be able to use Bai's arrest to my advantage."

He shook his head. "I would like to reach out to my superiors first. Joe Kingsley is a lieutenant now. We can ask him, or Rhy for that matter, to reach out to Marbury."

"No." She set her coffee aside, struggling to remain calm. "This is my op, not yours. I want to set up a meeting with Troy before we drag anyone else into this."

Their gazes clashed and held. They'd had some wonderful times together, but she knew they could both be stubborn.

Maybe too stubborn.

"Liana, you're not thinking through the implications," he began, but she abruptly cut him off.

"My operation, Brock, not yours." She threw up her hands in frustration. "And you wonder why Troy didn't want you involved? You're like a steamroller, blasting through anyone who dares stand in your way."

"That's not true. I'm a team player," he shot back.

"Maybe with your tactical team." She didn't lower her

gaze. "Not with us. And not when it comes to me being undercover."

He opened his mouth to argue but then took a sip of his coffee. She was impressed. Brock seemed to be holding back. She'd fully expected this discussion to end up in a full-blown argument.

"I'll set up the meeting with Troy in a neutral location. And maybe you can be hiding somewhere nearby." She hesitated, then added, "I never told Troy I was with you at the condo. Or that I met with you at PK's."

He looked surprised by that. "Maybe your disposable phone was tracked."

"Anything is possible." Disposable phones weren't easy to trace, but where there was a will, there was often a way. She drained her cup. "Troy is arranging for me to get a replacement vehicle. That works in our favor, as we'll have an untraceable vehicle to use."

"I don't know." Brock scowled, drumming his fingers on the table. "Maybe it's better to get something clean, with no ties to the department."

She knew Brock still didn't trust Troy. Yet his suggestion was valid, especially since she didn't know if she could salvage her cover. "We may need both. The type of car Troy will get fits in with my cover. But it may not have the same power a newer vehicle would."

"Then I say we get a clean vehicle first." Brock rose to his feet. "I can ask Rhy or Joe to get us a clean vehicle without telling them about you or the undercover op."

After mentally weighing the pros and cons, she nodded. "Okay, fine. But only if you promise not to tell them about me or the op."

"I promise." He looked relieved. "I'll make the call, see if Rhy or Joe can drop the vehicle here. You can hide in the bathroom. I'll just let them know I think I'm in danger."

Would two members of the upper brass of the tactical team buy that story? She wasn't convinced but decided to give it a try. She'd met both men at their wedding last April, which seemed like a lifetime ago. "Go ahead and call."

He hesitated, then pulled out his phone. "Rhy is closest; he lives in Brookland."

She listened as Brock made the call.

"Hey, Rhy, I need a favor. Well, two favors." Brock listened for a moment, then continued. "I need a personal leave of absence and a clean vehicle. Unfortunately, I think I'm in danger." Another pause. "Yes, I know there's a dead guy in my condo. Please don't ask, I can't give you details. At least not yet. I promise if things go south, you'll be my first call."

She wondered if Rhy would really let it go, and he must have because Brock's expression was one of relief.

"Yeah, I hear you. I know the team is there if I need you. Thanks. See you in thirty." He lowered the phone. "He's bringing a rental."

"In thirty minutes?" She arched a brow. "That's fast."

"Yeah, he's on a first-name basis with the manager of a local rental car company." He shrugged. "Rhy will make it happen."

"Okay." She rose and stretched. Then crossed over to make the bed she'd slept in. Best to hide the fact that there were two people here last night.

"We'll grab breakfast before we set up the meeting with Troy."

She straightened, pinning him with a narrow gaze. "Is that a suggestion or an order?"

He winced. "Suggestion. But one based on sound principle. If there's even the remote possibility your phone was tracked, better to make the call in a busy restaurant than from here."

Since she agreed with his rationale, she nodded. Working with Brock was already proving to be a challenge. When it came to work, it was his way or the highway.

She hadn't been interested in being a member of the tactical team. They were good cops, always the first sent in difficult situations. Then again, she hadn't been interested in working undercover either, yet here she was neck-deep in trouble.

They shared another pot of coffee. When Brock saw two SUVs pull into the parking lot, he shooed her into the bathroom. She gave the room one last look and realized there were two dirty coffee cups. Scooping one up, she ducked inside.

Their conversation was brief. Despite Rhy's subtle push for more information, Brock held his ground. When Rhy left, she joined Brock.

"How long before we can leave?"

"Let's give it ten minutes." He smiled for what seemed like the first time in eons. "Good catch on the second coffee cup."

"Thanks." She averted her gaze to hide her involuntary reaction to Brock's smile. He'd smiled a lot in the early days of their marriage. When they'd still basked in the glow of new love.

But it hadn't taken long for things to go horribly wrong.

After the allotted ten minutes, they left the motel. She was silent as Brock took a winding path back to the interstate.

"I'm hungry. How about we eat at the family restaurant up ahead?" she said, gesturing to the sign.

He nodded and exited the interstate. Sending him a sidelong glance, she wondered what he was thinking. That had been another problem in their brief marriage. Brock had kept everything to himself until things that were bothering him burst forth in a spat of anger.

The restaurant was nothing special, but the scent of bacon made her mouth water. She followed their hostess to a booth in the back.

After obtaining more coffee and placing their orders, she pulled her phone from her pocket. Brock reached out and put a hand on her arm. "Wait until we eat."

She swallowed a sigh. "It will take time for Troy to meet us here from the fourth district. Especially since I'm changing our original meeting."

"Please." His green gaze held hers.

"Fine. But the minute our food arrives, I'm calling. We can't sit here drinking coffee all morning."

"What's the plan once you have the replacement vehicle?"

She debated how much to tell him. "I'd like to check out the apartment where I've been living. See if anyone is watching the place."

"Okay. And where are you going to meet Troy to get the car?"

She glanced around the restaurant. "What's wrong with here? You can be outside in the SUV while I meet with Troy."

He didn't look thrilled but nodded. "I guess that will work."

Their meals arrived in record time. She picked up her phone and made the call. Troy answered on the second ring. "Where are you?"

"Grabbing breakfast." She gave him the restaurant

name and location. "Do you have the car? I know our original meeting was for ten, but things have changed. I need you to meet me here in thirty minutes."

"Understood, that's fine." Troy sounded relieved to hear from her. "I sent a uniform to your place, but he didn't see anyone lurking nearby. I had to pull him off to respond to another call."

"Okay. Did Bai give you anything yet?"

"No, but we need to discuss strategy. I may need you to chat with Bai."

"I can do that." Brock looked up with a frown at her words, but she ignored him. "See you soon." She disconnected from the call and dug into her French toast.

"Thirty minutes, huh?" Brock munched a piece of bacon.

"Yes." She was tempted to steal a slice the way she used to but held back. They didn't have that sort of relationship anymore.

The thought was depressing.

They ate in silence for several minutes. The time passed faster than she'd anticipated. Brock set his napkin on the table, pulled cash from his wallet, and left it on the table for their server.

"I'll hit the restroom, then head outside." He rose to his feet.

"Right behind you," she promised.

She lingered in the restroom, giving Brock plenty of time to get settled in the SUV outside. With five minutes left of the original thirty, she wove her way through the restaurant to head outside.

The sun was out, but the March wind was still cold. She huddled by the door for a moment, scanning the area out of habit more than concern.

A black sedan slowed in front of the entrance to the parking lot. She frowned. It looked too new to be a replacement for her rust bucket.

Her instincts went on high alert. Liana abruptly turned and dropped behind a large metal garbage can just as the crack of gunfire rang out for the second time in less than twelve hours.

CHAPTER FOUR

Having anticipated this very possibility, Brock already had his window down. He returned fire, shooting at the driver, then aiming for the tires and gas tank to incapacitate the vehicle.

Unlike the attempt at the condo, he wanted this guy in cuffs, not in the morgue.

Liana peeked out from the side of the garbage can, then darted toward the fallen gunman. Brock swallowed his protest, pushing out of the SUV to join her.

She lifted her gaze to his and slowly shook her head. "He's gone."

"How?" Brock knelt on the other side of the gunman. He'd aimed for his abdomen rather than his chest. But looking down, he could see blood spurting up from the abdominal wound like a bloody fountain.

"You must have struck his aortic artery." She rose, glancing around the parking lot. "We need to get out of here."

Brock nodded, understanding her concern. Restaurant patrons had their faces plastered up against the window, and some had their phones out. Those blasted phones were a pain in the behind. He took Liana's arm and hustled toward the SUV.

They hit the highway just as the wail of sirens filled the air.

"We need to call this in." He glanced at her. "I'd like to tell Rhy about what's going on. I understand you didn't want him to know about your role in the undercover operation, but we can't pretend we didn't kill two armed gunmen, one in the condo and one here. Especially since we know there were witnesses at the restaurant."

She nodded, her expression grim. "I don't like it, but you're right. We need to try to get ahead of this."

"You also need to ditch your phone." He never should have encouraged her to call Troy from the restaurant. "Troy is obviously dirty."

"You don't know that," she protested.

"Seriously?" He couldn't believe she was defending the guy. "You don't find it at all suspicious that minutes after you contact him, letting him know exactly where we are, a gunman shows up?"

She flushed and looked away. After a long moment, she rolled the window down and tossed the disposable cell phone. It bounced against the concrete road and shattered into pieces.

He wrestled his temper under control, relieved she'd gone along with the plan. He pulled out his cell phone. He used the facial recognition to unlock the screen, then thumbed to Rhy's number.

"What's going on, Brock?" Rhy asked.

"A lot," he admitted. "Look, can you meet us somewhere?"

"Us?" Rhy echoed.

"Yeah." He glanced at Liana, then added, "I'm with Liana. She's been working an operation, but her cover has been blown. We just killed another gunman outside a family restaurant."

Rhy let out a low whistle. "Yeah, I think we should meet at the City Central Hotel. I'll arrange for a suite. Say thirty minutes?"

"City Central works. But can you bring a set of disposable phones too?"

"Yes, that's not a problem," Rhy agreed.

"Thanks." He ended the call and lowered his phone.

"You need to get rid of your phone too." Liana gave him a pointed look. "Your condo was broken into, remember? Whoever is leaking intel knows we're together."

He hated to admit she was right. With a sigh, he powered down the phone and then tossed it out his window. Good thing he'd asked for a pair of phones.

"Why are we meeting at the City Central Hotel?" she asked.

"It's as good a place as any." He glanced at her. "Rhy is getting a suite. We need a plan moving forward."

"Funny, that's exactly what Troy said." She blew out a breath. "It doesn't make sense that he's behind these attacks. Why would he bother to send someone after me now? This all started after you walked into the kitchen at Lu Chen's."

It burned to know she still trusted Troy, despite the most recent attack. "Yes, I admit that's my fault. However, you contacted Troy several times, each of those calls coinciding with an attack. Frankly, I don't know what additional evidence you need. It's as clear as daylight that he's involved."

"Maybe it's not Troy but someone above him," she

murmured. "Captain Marbury or maybe even someone else."

"A good handler wouldn't tell anyone else," he shot back. "That's why these operations have a point person."

She fell silent, digesting his words. He told himself not to take her steadfast defense of Troy personally. But it was difficult not to.

He got off the interstate and backtracked, just to be sure they weren't followed. He didn't trust the guy as far as he could spit, especially not with Liana's life.

They arrived at the City Central Hotel exactly thirty minutes after his call with Rhy. When they checked in at the front desk, the clerk handed them two room keys for a suite on the first floor.

"Thanks," he said with a nod. He was familiar with the suites and quickly accessed the room to find Rhy sitting inside, sipping coffee.

"Brock. Liana." Rhy set his cup aside and rose to his feet. "I've put the precinct following up on the restaurant shooting on alert that officers were involved. But they're going to need to talk to both of you soon."

He grimaced and nodded. "I understand."

"I can't," Liana said firmly. "Not yet."

Rhy arched a brow, then gestured to the seating area. "Let's talk. I admit, I was surprised to hear about this undercover operation you've been involved in, Liana."

"You're not supposed to know about it." Her tone was testy as she dropped onto the sofa. "That's the whole point of being undercover."

Brock shrugged at Rhy's questioning look. "Obviously, it was news to me too."

Rhy pursed his lips for a moment. "Liana, I understand your reluctance to speak with the local cops about the restaurant incident. But there's also the dead guy at Brock's condo. Do you really expect him to take the brunt of both events?"

She slowly shook her head. "No, of course not. It's just —I don't want to give up my goal of uncovering the identity of the man responsible for the largest sex-trafficking organization in the state."

"We want to find him too," Brock reassured her. "I'm sure the best way to do that is by working together."

"You don't understand." Liana looked frustrated. "I can't go into a situation with a slew of cops hovering nearby. I may only have one more shot at this. And for that, I'll need to meet with my contact alone."

"You can't be serious," Brock blurted. "That's a suicide mission."

"One chance," Liana repeated. "If this doesn't work, then we'll have little choice but to move on to a plan B."

"What can you tell us about this sex-trafficking ring?" Rhy asked. "There must be something we can do on our end to find those involved."

"I've put four months of work in on this," she said in a low tone. "Months of wiggling my way up in the organization. I've only met my contact twice; he's extremely cautious."

Brock was frustrated with the lack of information. "And what's your contact's name?"

"Muchin." She shrugged. "I don't know if that's a first name or last name or an alias of some sort. I only know him as Muchin."

The name meant nothing to Brock. He glanced at Rhy, who looked just as clueless. "I've never heard of him," Rhy said.

"Troy ran the name through the database but didn't get

a hit." She hesitated, then added, "I learned the leader of the sex-trafficking ring is a man only known as Twisted Snake. My objective is to uncover his true identity."

"Sounds like something out of a low-budget movie," Rhy muttered.

Brock tended to agree. "And you're sure that Muchin and Twisted Snake are not one and the same man?"

"I'm positive," Liana said quickly. "The only thing I know about Twisted Snake is that he has several snake tattoos along his arms, hence the nickname."

"Maybe Muchin has snake tattoos in places you haven't seen," Brock felt compelled to point out.

"Muchin has tattoos, a skull on one arm, crossed swords on the other. No snakes. And I doubt he has them hidden, otherwise the nickname wouldn't have stuck." She waved an impatient hand. "Muchin is very protective of Twisted Snake. He carries out Twisted Snake's orders without question. I'm sure they are not the same person."

"Okay, so Muchin is a mid-level player in the organization," Rhy said. "Where does Bai Chow fit in?"

"He was my partner in getting girls," she admitted. "He got the girls, and I took care of placing them. Instead of placing them in prostitution, though, I got them out of there, handing them over to Troy in exchange for cash that I returned to Bai for services rendered. But he had others working for him, too. Those girls are still out there."

"What if Troy just moved the girls to another location?" Brock asked.

"I know they got out because I followed up with them afterward." She narrowed her gaze. "And that's why I know Troy isn't dirty."

"You don't know that," Brock snapped.

"Let's get back to the operation," Rhy suggested, eyeing

them as if worried they'd come to blows. Brock had never raised a hand to a woman in his life, and he wasn't going to start now. "You're saying Bai Chow used the restaurant as a front for getting the girls?"

"It was more his attempt to look legitimate, although I did learn that they often brought women in from China allegedly to work the restaurant, only to end up being sex trafficked." She frowned. "I hated to learn one of my favorite restaurants was a front for sex trafficking. I was able to save a dozen girls, but there are more, so many more that I couldn't pull out of there."

For a moment, a heavy silence fell between them. Brock didn't much like learning the restaurant was a front for prostitution either. "A dozen girls is impressive, Liana. I'm sure they are grateful for your help."

She frowned. "Maybe, but it's a drop in the bucket compared to what I suspect is still going on. If we can get to Twisted Snake, I'm convinced we'll save many more."

"I understand." He exchanged a glance with Rhy. "What can we do to help?"

Liana turned to look at him. "I need you and Rhy to step aside and allow me to take the lead on setting up a meeting with Muchin."

He didn't want to give in. Didn't like having to agree to let her make the decisions on how to proceed on this. Yet she had spent four months of her life on this operation. Liana knew the players better than anyone.

"Okay." He forced the word past his tight throat. "I promise you can take the lead on this moving forward."

Rhy nodded slowly. "I'll go along with that too. But I would like you to keep us in the loop, Liana. Your life is on the line. It won't help any of those victims you weren't able to rescue if those running this organization succeed in killing you."

She grimaced. "Yes, I know. Trust me, that's not what I want either. I don't have a death wish, but I may be able to shift the blame for the police showing up at the restaurant on Bai Chow, securing my place within the sex-trafficking operation."

Brock wanted to trust her, yet it wasn't easy. Even though he could admit he was wrong about her relationship with Troy, she'd still walked away. And had kept secrets from him.

And for all he knew, she still was.

THE SUSPICION in Brock's green eyes was difficult to ignore. She hadn't done anything to deserve his mistrust. Well, that wasn't true, she was forced to silently admit. She had left him to take this assignment.

But she had never cheated on him. The way he'd accused her of doing.

Brock worked with several beautiful, single women on his tactical team. Raelyn, Jina, and Cassidy were all stunning. She knew he worked closely with them in dangerous situations. Yet she never assumed their closeness meant they were sleeping together. Was it wrong to expect the same courtesy from him?

Apparently.

Whatever. There was no point in rehashing what had gone wrong between them. Water under the bridge. Maybe it had been nice to have Brock backing her up when the gunman opened fire outside the restaurant, but that was work.

He would do the same for any police officer.

"I'm in agreement of letting Liana take the lead on this," Rhy said. "But I insist you have at least one or two cops backing you up." When she opened her mouth to protest, Rhy lifted his hand. "This is not open for discussion. There have been two recent attempts to kill you. I think we have to assume any meeting you set up is likely to be a trap."

She looked from Rhy to Brock. Both men had steely determination in their eyes. She reluctantly nodded. "Fine, but only if they are well out of sight."

The flash of relief in Brock's gaze was gone so fast she may have imagined it. "I think we need to speak with Bai Chow," Brock said. "Using your knowledge of his role in this, we may be able to force his cooperation."

She'd had the same thought. And Troy had mentioned that too. She had to think for a moment, glancing at the clock on the microwave. Time had been moving at warp speed. "It's Thursday, right? He should have his arraignment hearing in court this morning."

"Yes." Brock seemed to pick up her thought process. "Rhy, can you have him brought to our precinct after his court hearing?"

"I'll pull some strings," he agreed. "The sheriff's department arranges for transporting prisoners to and from the jail to the courthouse. Too bad Kyleigh is on light desk duty because of her pregnancy, or I could ask her for help on this." Rhy rose and pulled out his phone, moving to the other side of the room to make his call.

Brock stood, too, and crossed over to open the plastic bag on the table. He pulled out two disposable phones, showing them to her. "Let's get these up and running."

"Okay." She joined him at the table. "Good thing I have Muchin's number memorized."

He nodded. "I figured you did, or you wouldn't have tossed your phones so quickly."

It felt nice to be working together, even if it was only a temporary arrangement. The conversation between Rhy and whoever he was talking to within the sheriff's department ended rather quickly.

"Bai Chow's arraignment was postponed until tomorrow." Rhy shrugged. "Some problem within the public defender's office."

She was disappointed but wasn't going to let that minor setback derail her plan. "I'll set up the meeting with Muchin anyway. He'll likely hold off returning my call until later this evening, regardless of what time I contact him. He always sets up meetings at night as if instinctively avoiding any chance of being seen."

"You think he'll agree to meet with you despite knowing of Bai's arrest?" Brock asked.

"I think so, yes." She glanced at him. "Although, as Rhy pointed out, it could very well be a trap."

"Then why even try?" Brock scowled. "There's no point in placing yourself in danger."

"I can't turn my back on those girls. If there's a remote chance this will work, I need to take it." She hesitated, then added, "There is one more thing you probably should know. My cousin Mai Shi has been missing for the past four months. There's a strong possibility that she was taken by Bai."

"So that's why you threw caution to the wind to take this undercover operation," Brock said.

"I didn't throw caution to the wind." Would Brock feel the same way if some other female cop had taken the role? She doubted it. This was about her. "I accepted an undercover assignment. One that is important to me."

"How do you know your cousin has been caught in the sex-trafficking operation?" Rhy asked, his tone reasonable.

"Mai Shi was working at the restaurant before she disappeared." She sighed. "I hardly think that's a coincidence."

"There were a few females working in the kitchen last night," Brock said with a frown. "Why haven't they been taken away?"

"The women must be pleasing to the eye, at least according to Bai. You may have noticed they tend to wear face masks to hide bad teeth or bad skin." She shivered. "Trust me, I was fortunate that I was able to maintain my position within the organization without being drugged and taken away."

There was another impossibly long silence as Rhy and Brock stared at her in shock.

"I'm glad God has been watching over you, Liana," Rhy finally said. "But this is a very dangerous situation. I'm surprised your precinct didn't look for a man to infiltrate the organization."

"They chose me because I can speak Chinese and because I can blend into the organization better than anyone else." She was tired of trying to prove herself worthy. She was a good cop and could take care of herself, no matter what they thought. "I'm sorry that you feel I'm not up to the task."

"I didn't say that," Rhy chided. "It's just that you're in a vulnerable position, more so than what other undercover cops might experience."

"I'm aware," she said, gritting her teeth from snapping at him. "But I played my role very well for months."

Until Brock blew her cover. She didn't say the words, but they hung in the air between them as if she had.

"I need to get back to the precinct," Rhy said after a long moment. "You should be safe here. I only ask that you keep me posted on the details of your meeting with Muchin, so we can make sure to have at least one officer, if not two, staked out nearby."

"Sure." She turned away, not wanting to admit that Muchin wasn't stupid, he wouldn't give her much lead time in getting to a meeting. Even less so now that Bai had been arrested. "Brock is here. He can back me up."

"I'll be there no matter what," Brock said. "But it wouldn't hurt to have another officer or two stationed nearby."

"Whatever we can arrange is fine." She decided there was no point in arguing. She couldn't even be sure Muchin would agree to a meeting, much less show up.

And if he didn't? She hid a wince. She didn't want to admit she hadn't gotten nearly as much intel during her four months of working undercover as she would have liked.

There was one other possible option, but she'd hold off on that until later. If Muchin had believed her when she'd called him after Bai's arrest, he would want to talk about how they would fill the gap.

She'd hoped that would mean she'd take over Bai's role. It would get her one step closer to uncovering the truth of Twisted Snake's identity and where he could be found.

The door closed behind Rhy with a soft click. Brock slid the dead bolt home, then turned to face her. "I wish you would have told me about your cousin."

"I wish a lot of things." She crossed over to drop onto the sofa cushion. The brief sense of teamwork she'd experienced with him earlier seemed to have vanished. "What difference would it have made? My reasons shouldn't matter. The biggest problem was that Troy didn't want you involved in the operation."

"If I had been, I wouldn't have walked into the kitchen at Lu Chen's," he said.

"Seriously?" She stared at him. "You really think you would have just stayed quiet for months while I infiltrated the organization? No way, Brock. There is absolutely no way you would have done that."

He flushed and nodded, crossing over to join her on the sofa. "Okay, that may be true. I still wish you would have been honest with me about why you took this operation."

She turned so that her back was tucked into the corner, putting a bit of distance between them. "Look, Brock, rehashing the past isn't going to get us anywhere. There's no point. What's done is done."

He stared at her for a long moment, then looked away. "Yeah. You're right. We can't change the past."

They could possibly change the future, but she didn't say the words. For months she'd walked a narrow tightrope, playing her role within the organization, staying alive and saving girls from being forced into prostitution.

Sitting in the hotel suite with Brock was like walking a fine line between the present and the past. She couldn't afford to think about whether or not they had a future together once this was over.

"Rhy is big on God and faith," Brock said, surprising her. "Recently, I've attended a few church services with them."

His comment surprised her. "It sounds like you're starting to believe."

"I guess I am," Brock admitted. "Looking back over everything that has happened, it sure seems as if this is all part of God's plan."

"It doesn't make sense to me that God would put my cousin Mai Shi in harm's way."

"I know. It's not always easy to understand why we are placed in difficult situations," he agreed. "Yet we're alive, Liana. And I promise to help you find Twisted Snake and your cousin Mai Shi."

"I—thank you." She was humbled by his sincerity.

"I need to call Raelyn and Grayson, let them know that we may need back up." He surprised her by reaching over to take her hand in his. "I trust you to take the lead on meeting Muchin but would ask that you trust me and the rest of the tactical team to back you up. I promise he won't know we're there."

"I do trust you to back me up." She stared at their joined hands, savoring the warmth. Then it was gone as Brock stood and used one of the new phones to make the call.

Listening to him talk to Raelyn about the plan made her realize how nice it must be to work closely with a team of cops. She'd always had a partner, but what Brock had was different.

It was clear he trusted his teammates to chip in at any time of the day or night as needed. And she was glad Brock intended to be there for her, no matter how this mission unfolded.

She only wished he'd offered the same support and understanding during their brief marriage.

CHAPTER FIVE

After discussing options with Raelyn and Grayson, Brock slipped the disposable phone back into his pocket. He hadn't realized Liana's cousin was missing, likely by the sex traffickers. It made more sense now why she had thrown herself into this assignment.

He just wished she'd told him the truth.

There was no denying he'd jumped to conclusions without any real evidence. And he needed to own that. He shouldn't have been so eager to believe the worst about her meeting with Troy.

A text message. Had he really thrown his marriage away over a text message? It wasn't even a sexy text message. Just a brief exchange between the two of them agreeing to meet the following morning. In the daytime.

If she'd been texting with a woman, he wouldn't have thought twice about it.

"Something wrong?" Liana frowned. "You look upset."

He was upset with himself for being an idiot. "I'm fine." He managed a smile. "What time are you calling Muchin?"

She looked thoughtful. "Now." She shrugged. "He

won't answer the phone anyway since it's an unknown number."

He listened as she made contact with Muchin.

"Muchin, this is Feng." Her voice vibrated with fear, and he had to admit she was doing a good job of submersing herself into her undercover role. "Bai allowed the police to find him, and they are searching for me too. I need to see you in person. Please call me." After a brief pause, she added in Chinese, "I fear Bai cannot be trusted."

When she ended the call, he nodded. "I hope you hear from him soon."

"He's usually good about returning calls. Especially those that may impact his business." She scowled. "I don't know that he'll agree to a meeting, though. He might be too on edge to go that far."

Brock didn't like the sound of that. "We need something to go on."

"Tell me about it." She stared down at the phone in her hands, then lifted her gaze to his. "I think we should head to my apartment."

Her apartment? The place she'd been living for the past four months without him? He kept his tone even with an effort. "Why do you need to go there?"

"The apartment is part of my cover as Feng Chi. It's on the north side, in one of the worst areas of the city." She tapped the phone into the palm of her hand. "I'm curious if someone from the Twisted Snake organization is watching the place. Could be they're looking for another opportunity to take me out."

His knee-jerk reaction was to refuse to go anywhere near the place. But then he reminded himself that he'd promised to help. "And if someone is watching the place? Then what?"

She held his gaze. "He'll try to attack me, and we'll grab him. We'll take him to the precinct to book him for assault, see if we can get him to talk. It's highly likely he'll have at least one weapon on him, probably two—a gun and a knife. And he also could have outstanding warrants."

He didn't love the idea, especially the part about waiting for the guy to grab her, but it was better than sitting around doing nothing. He nodded. "Okay, I'm in."

"Great. The biggest problem is that we need a junker car." She frowned. "Rhy's SUV is a magnet for trouble. It will either get stolen or be pegged as belonging to a cop. No one drives anything that nice in the area where I've been staying."

Again, he could see her point about needing a different car. He thought about his teammates for a moment. Zeke had two cars, an older sedan and a four-wheel-drive truck. Zeke had kept the sedan because the truck guzzled gas. "I have a buddy who has an older sedan we can borrow. If you agree," he added, "I'll call him."

Her dark eyes brightened. "That would be great."

He almost laughed at the idea of Liana being so excited at having access to an old car, but the danger that loomed before them was too serious. She made this trip to her apartment sound easy when it was anything but.

It took a moment for him to recall Zeke Hawthorn's number from memory. He placed the call, which of course went to voice mail. Nobody answered unknown numbers these days, and he didn't blame Zeke. He left a brief message, then ended the call. He'd give Zeke ten minutes before going up the chain of command.

Thankfully, Zeke called back in five. "What's going on?" Zeke demanded. "Where's your phone?"

"Shattered into pieces somewhere outside of Brookland. Listen, I need a favor. Can I borrow your Ford Taurus?"

"You know it's twelve years old, right?" Zeke sounded perplexed. "Why don't you get a set of wheels from someone else?"

"I need something older, like your Taurus." Brock didn't want to get into details about their plan.

"Yeah, sure. It's at my place. I'll give you the code to get into the garage. Keys are on the hook in the kitchen."

"Thanks, buddy." Brock was relieved. "I appreciate your help on this."

"Something going on that you need to tell us about?" Zeke asked suspiciously. "We heard you're on personal leave. You know we're here for you if needed."

"I may need to bring you in, but not now. We'll talk about it later, okay?" Brock was anxious to get to Zeke's for the sedan. "Thanks again."

"No problem. Be safe out there," Zeke cautioned, before ending the call.

He reached for his coat. "Let's go." He was about to suggest they get a rideshare but then realized they only had disposable phones with no rideshare apps on them. "I'll ask the front desk to call for a taxi. That way we don't have to backtrack here to drop off the SUV."

"Works for me." She reached for her thin jacket. "Where does he live?"

"Greenland." He reached for the door. "Shouldn't take too long to get there."

The longest part of the trip was waiting for the taxi to arrive. Since the evolution of rideshares, the taxi business had dwindled, which resulted in longer wait times. After twenty-five minutes of waiting, the taxi rolled up. From there, it took another fifteen minutes to get to Zeke's house.

Striding to the garage door keypad, he entered the code. The two-car garage door rumbled open, revealing the nondescript Ford Taurus. "Hang on, I'll grab the keys."

Liana frowned. "I was hoping it would be in worse shape."

"At least it's not new." He ducked into the house and grabbed the keys. Soon they were back on the road.

When Liana gave him her address, he did his best not to show his horror. She hadn't been kidding when she'd mentioned staying in the worst part of the city. It made him angry all over again at how she'd willingly placed herself in harm's way for this assignment.

Yes, she wanted to find her cousin. He could understand that. But there had to be other ways to accomplish that without working within the sex-trafficking organization.

"I know what you're thinking," she said, breaking the strained silence. "No one forced me to take this job."

That only made it worse. Yet he managed to hold back. "It's a rough area to have a woman staying in an apartment all alone."

"I'm aware. But I'm also a well-trained cop."

She was, but he still didn't like it. Swallowing another argument, he focused on navigating the side streets to get to the north side. "We'll probably need to find a place to park and go the rest of the way on foot."

"Yep. That's one of the reasons having an older car is so important. I always had to park several blocks away from the apartment building." She shrugged. "I could never be one hundred percent certain my car would be there when I returned."

Brock ended up driving past the apartment building first to check the place out. It looked worse than he'd imagined. He felt sick to his stomach imagining Liana staying there for any length of time.

He knew he needed to get his overprotective instincts under control. And soon. As he made a loop around the block, searching for a parking space, he saw a drug deal going down on the corner. And a little farther down, a woman dressed in thigh-high boots, a short skirt, and a fake fur coat climbed into the passenger seat of a car.

This part of the city wasn't within his precinct's jurisdiction, and while he knew it wasn't fair, he wanted to drive straight over to the third district captain on duty to give the upper brass a piece of his mind. There was criminal activity going on in broad daylight and not a squad to be seen.

"Try the next block," Liana said, breaking into his thoughts. "I often have luck finding spots there."

Much of their recent snowfall had melted, but there were still snowbanks on the sides of the streets, making it difficult to navigate around other parked cars. It made the back of his neck itch to drive this slowly through the narrow streets, knowing there were likely illegal guns in just about every house.

Okay, not all of them, but far too many for his peace of mind.

Three blocks later, he found a spot. He'd barely gotten the Taurus parallel parked into the opening when his phone rang.

"Greer," he answered.

"It's Raelyn." His teammate's voice sounded strained. "I'm afraid I have bad news."

He glanced at Liana who was obviously listening. "What kind of bad news?"

"Bai Chow was just found dead in his cell."

"Bai Chow is dead? How? Don't they have cameras watching these guys twenty-four seven?"

"They do," Raelyn conceded. "There's an investigation underway. All we know for sure is that he fell to the ground in what appeared to be a seizure." She sighed. "Our working theory is that he was drugged. Either by another inmate or by one of the guards."

"Drugged." He glanced at Liana. "How soon will they do the autopsy?"

"It's scheduled for first thing in the morning, but tox screens take time. Those results won't be in for at least two weeks, maybe longer."

"Yeah, that figures." He didn't like this turn of events one bit. "I'm willing to bet they'll find the cameras weren't working during this timeframe either."

"We have the feds involved," Raelyn said. "They've already asked for all of the camera footage."

"Thanks, Rae." He lowered the phone.

"I doubt they'll find anything on the video," Liana said in a low voice. "This has to be an inside job."

"I know." He reached over to take her hand. "We should have pushed to talk to him sooner."

She surprised him by gripping his fingers tightly. "I don't know that he would have cooperated anyway."

"Maybe not," he agreed. But it would have been worth a shot.

And now they'd never know what, if anything, Bai Chow might have told them.

LIANA WAS DEPRESSED over Bai Chow's murder. There wasn't a doubt in her mind that Twisted Snake had paid someone to kill Bai before he could talk.

And there was no denying she was likely the next on the chopping block. This was one of the reasons it was so difficult to identify the man responsible for the sex-trafficking operation. Twisted Snake didn't hesitate to kill those he suspected of double crossing him. The lure of easy money was such that he would just find someone else to take over.

The meeting with Muchin—if there was one—would need to be handled with caution. She didn't want to die, but at the same time, she couldn't bear the thought of failing in her mission to find Mai Shi.

"Liana?" She turned to look at Brock. He was watching her intently. "Are you okay?"

"Yes." She had to put this setback aside. "Ready to head out to the apartment?"

"It's not too late to call this whole thing off," he said in a low voice. "If Muchin arranged for Bai to be murdered, you're next on the list."

"I know that's a possibility. But I'm not calling anything off. Not yet." She thought for a moment. "You said yourself that we need a lead. I'd like you to stay here in the sedan for a few minutes while I head out. Just showing my face might bring someone out of hiding."

"Anyone watching for you will try to kill you."

She couldn't deny it. "I'll be ready. And you'll be there to back me up. You remember my apartment number, right?"

"Yeah. I remember."

"Good." She gently pulled her hand from his and pushed open her door. "Give me two minutes." She smiled, then slid out of the vehicle. Slamming the door shut, she tucked her chin down and hid her hands in her pockets, feeling the weight of her weapon hidden there as she walked quickly toward the next corner.

There wasn't anyone outside on the street, but the hairs on the back of her neck were standing on end as if she was being watched from one of the many windows of the dilapidated houses lining the street.

Despite her brave attitude in the face of Brock's doubt, she didn't like feeling vulnerable. She wasn't afraid of hand-to-hand combat, but she could easily be shot in the back at any point along the street.

And the neighbors would pretend nothing had happened.

As she turned the corner, she heard the soft thud of a car door closing. Brock was on his way. Using her peripheral vision, she zeroed in on movement from the right. A woman tossed a bag of garbage into the closest can, then disappeared back inside.

False alarm.

The trip to her apartment seemed to take forever, but she soon covered the six blocks. There was no sign of anyone hanging around outside the apartment building, and the drug dealer had moved on too.

So far, so good.

She mounted the steps to the building. The security lock was broken, so she wrenched the door open and stepped inside. A large, heavily tattooed white man came down the stairs, straight toward her.

In her pocket, her fingers closed around the gun.

She lifted her chin, meeting his gaze straight on. He stared back, raking his gaze over her, as if she were a fresh slab of meat, but he didn't make a move toward her. Stepping aside, she gave him plenty of room to move past.

He left the building without saying a word. Not entirely surprising. This wasn't the sort of place where you borrowed sugar from your neighbor across the hall. It was best not to talk to anyone in the building. Like, ever.

Breathing a sigh of relief, she headed up the stairs to her second-floor apartment. The big tattooed man didn't look familiar, and she found herself praying he wasn't involved in this mess. If he turned around and came back after her, she was in trouble.

Fighting him would not be easy.

Like the night before, she paused to listen outside her doorway before using the key to get inside. She pushed the door open, half expecting a barrage of gunfire.

There was nothing but silence.

She edged over the threshold, pressing her back against the wall. Then she performed a quick search, making sure no one was hiding inside.

Another quick glance around the room confirmed no one had been here since last night. Or if someone had come inside, they hadn't searched her things.

Still, she kept her guard up, every sense on alert. Hearing footsteps from the hallway, she checked the peephole. Seeing Brock, she opened the door to let him in.

"Wow, what happened to the neat freak I married?" he asked, eyeing the disarray.

"It's a planned mess." She shut the door behind him. "Helps me know if anyone has been inside."

"Really?" He arched a brow. "Seems counterintuitive."

"It's not. If the place was spotless, with everything neatly in its place, that's how an intruder would leave it.

With a mess, they don't bother to be as precise, assuming I'll never figure it out."

"You're the expert." He glanced around again. "I guess I can see your logic."

She bit back a sarcastic reply. Maybe she wasn't an expert at working undercover, but she'd been at it for months now, so he could give her a little credit.

"Who was that guy who came out of the building?" Brock asked, changing the subject. "Any chance that's Twisted Snake?"

She frowned. "I'm not sure who he was. He didn't look familiar. But he could have been visiting someone. Or our paths hadn't crossed until now. I don't think he's Twisted Snake, though. I've been led to believe Twisted Snake is from the Triad. That would make him Chinese, not Caucasian."

He nodded. "Does the fact that you were able to get here safely mean you're off the hook?"

"Got me." She had no idea what it meant. "We should stay here for a bit, though. I don't want to leave too soon."

He nodded and dropped onto the sofa that was partially covered with laundry. She couldn't sit still, though, moving from window to window to look outside at the neighborhood below.

"The drug dealer is back," she said in a low voice. "I see him there a lot."

"You should have notified the police."

"That's not how to blend in here, Brock." She rolled her eyes. "It's far better for these people to believe I'm hiding from the cops as much as they are."

"Oh, yeah." He looked chagrined. "That makes sense."

"For your information, I did make an anonymous call about the drug dealer." She turned back to the window.

"But if the precinct sent anyone out, I didn't see them. And clearly, the drug dealer isn't worried about being caught."

"I know. It's bugging me too," he admitted. "I'm sure they have bigger crimes to deal with, but a patrol through the area on occasion would be helpful."

"I have only seen the rare squad on patrol, but they do respond to gunfire." She shrugged, glancing back over her shoulder at him. "That's something."

"Not enough." Brock's flash of anger was quickly subdued. "Sorry. I'm on edge."

Sorry? Brock rarely apologized. It was so strange to be working this closely with him. They'd always worked out of different precincts, having met at Paulie's Pub, one of the local cop hangouts. There was an unwritten rule about married cops working out of the same house, which she'd always thought was pretty smart. As a female cop, it was hard enough to earn the respect from the guys around her. If she'd have worked with Brock, his overprotectiveness would have ruined her image.

She managed a smile. "It's okay. I've been on edge for months now."

"I can only imagine."

She turned back toward the window, then abruptly straightened. "He's back."

"Who, the drug dealer?" Brock rose and crossed over to stand beside her.

"No, big Tattoo Guy," she said as she watched the large white man stroll down the street toward the apartment building. His hands were tucked into his pockets, much the way hers had been.

Did he have a weapon too? Very likely.

"I don't like this," Brock muttered. "We need to get out of here."

"It's too late now to go out the front." She moved to the side of the window. "Take up a position at the other window."

Brock did so, pulling his weapon from its holster. She removed her gun too. The beefy guy paused on the street corner for a moment, then looked up, directly toward her apartment windows.

He was there for her. She inwardly railed at herself for deciding to stay.

"He won't be easy to take down," Brock said, stating the obvious.

"No kidding." She stayed where she was, watching as the tattooed man continued toward the building.

The minute he was out of sight, the angle from the windows made it impossible for her to see the front door, she moved away from the window. "Let's go. Down the hall to my room."

Brock followed without question, understanding the very real possibility the tattooed man would simply spray her apartment door with bullets. It wasn't as if the bedroom was that much safer.

Yet there was an escape route. Not exactly subtle in daylight, but better than becoming a bull's-eye.

"We need to call for backup," Brock whispered.

"Don't be ridiculous. There isn't time for that." She shot him an exasperated glance over her shoulder. After tucking her gun back into her coat pocket, she headed for the window air conditioner and began pulling it free.

"What are you doing?" Brock hesitated only a moment before holstering his gun, too, and pitching in to help.

"Getting us out of here." Between the two of them, they set the window air conditioner aside. She peered out the opening, glancing down. It was a second-story window, which wasn't optimal.

But it was their only option.

She slung her leg over the windowsill.

"Wait a minute, you'll break a leg dropping down that far," Brock protested.

"It's possible, yes. But I've done this before without a problem." The words were barely out of her mouth when a large crashing sound reached her ears.

Not bullets. The big tattooed man had simply kicked in the front door to her apartment.

She ducked under the window and lowered herself over the edge until just her hands were gripping the lower sill. Then she let go, dropping to the ground with a jarring thud. She twisted her ankle, but it wasn't bad enough to worry about.

Glancing up, she saw Brock crawl through the window, following her lead. He was larger across the shoulders, so it took him a few seconds longer.

"Hurry," she whispered, moving back against the wall of the building, well out of the way. She glanced around, hoping they weren't being watched. The tattooed guy could have had someone else stationed back here to watch for them.

Brock dropped next to her.

"This way." She took the lead, knowing the area better than he did. She lightly ran along the side of the building toward the narrow opening between the apartment building and the house next door.

They'd barely reached the corner when gunfire erupted from behind them. A quick glance over her shoulder confirmed Tattoo Guy was firing his weapon at them from her bedroom window.

CHAPTER SIX

"Go, go!" Brock covered Liana as much as possible as the large tattooed guy opened fire. His heart thudded against his ribs as they ducked around the corner between the two buildings. He inwardly railed at himself for not anticipating this.

He hated knowing Liana was in danger. Anger wasn't useful, though, so he did his best to battle it back. He followed Liana through one of the worst neighborhoods in the city, knowing another gunman could pop up at any moment.

A silent yet urgent prayer asking for God to protect them flashed in his mind. Rhy, Joe, and Steele were rubbing off on him.

And right now, he and Liana needed all the help they could get.

After what seemed like an hour, but was really only fifteen minutes, Liana headed in the direction of Zeke's Ford sedan. He scoured the area, searching for anyone paying them too much attention, but he didn't see anything suspicious. As they approached the sedan, he put a hand on Liana's arm to hold her back.

"I want to check it out first," he whispered.

"Check out what?" She frowned. "We need to get out of here."

Last month, a bomb had been placed beneath the SUV Steele had been using while keeping his now fiancée safe. He didn't plan on making the same mistake. They'd been gone from the vehicle long enough for an explosive device or a GPS tracker to be planted.

"Keep watch. This won't take long." He ran his fingers along the rear bumper, then the wheel wells. Then he stretched out on the ground and edged beneath the vehicle. He wished he had a flashlight, but he was forced to use his hands, running them over the entire undercarriage to get the job done.

"Hurry," Liana urged.

He stretched his long arms out and confirmed there was nothing planted beneath the sedan. Then he wiggled out from the vehicle, his hands covered in grease.

"I'll drive," Liana said. "Keys?"

He dug them from his pocket, then ran to the other side to get in. Noticing a discarded hoodie in the back seat, he stretched out and grabbed it. As he used it to clean his hands, he made a mental note to buy Zeke another one.

Thirty seconds later, they were on the road. Liana took several turns, following a route that was only in her mind. He kept a keen eye out for danger as they went from one street of dilapidated houses to the next.

"I'm sorry," she finally said, when they were safely far enough away from her apartment to relax a bit. "This is my fault. I shouldn't have stayed at the apartment after passing Tattoo Guy on the stairs."

"You had no way of knowing he was one of the bad guys." He reached out to touch her hand. "I feel like I'm the one who failed you."

"You didn't." She shot him a quick glance before turning back to the road. "I guess he was the one watching my place. Maybe I caught him off guard by coming in as he was leaving."

He thought about that. "I'm surprised he didn't grab you then."

"That's one of the reasons I didn't view him as much of a threat." She sighed. "I was wrong."

"Or maybe he was only told to watch the place, but not to approach you." Brock remembered he'd passed the guy on the street too. "He may have called his contact who then told him to take you out of the picture."

"That makes sense." She frowned. "Although now they know about you."

He turned to face her. "That's good. I'm glad they know you're not alone."

She fell silent, taking the on-ramp to the interstate. "Now that my cover is blown, there's no way Muchin will call me back."

"You don't know where he lives?"

"No. He set up meetings outside most of the time, often within blocks of Lu Chen's."

"Maybe we should get a search warrant for the restaurant."

"After Bai's arrest, they'll have removed anything that may have been useful." She shrugged. "Besides, they're trafficking women, not drugs. I never saw any girls gathered together at the restaurant itself. That's just where I connected with Bai to make payments."

"Yeah." He didn't like it, but she was probably right.

She made an abrupt left turn, heading east. He quickly understood her destination. "You're heading to the restaurant now?"

"It may be worth it for us to watch the place. I should have considered this sooner, but the main cook—they don't use titles like chef and sous chef—was a man named Dong."

"No last name?"

"I wasn't formally introduced," she said in a dry tone. "But he was there the night you barged into the kitchen. And he may even be next in line to take over as manager in Bai's absence if I'm also out of the picture. I think we should find him and see if we can get him to talk."

"Okay, that works." He couldn't argue her logic. Danger dogged their footsteps, and the best way to get rid of the gunmen following her was to find the man known as Twisted Snake.

And to do that, they needed information.

"If we're going to be staking out the restaurant, we need equipment," he told her. "Specifically binoculars."

"True." She hesitated. "Where should we get them? A sporting goods store?"

Since heading back to his condo was out of the question, he nodded. "Yes, there's a sporting goods store relatively close. The army surplus store is on the other side of town, and there's no guarantee we'll find what we need." He eyed her thin coat critically. "And warmer clothes would be good too."

"You'll have to give me directions."

He guided her back to the interstate, then to a huge sporting goods store. It was the sort of place that catered to deer hunters, a major sport in Wisconsin. Personally, he'd never understood the allure. Maybe because he spent his days hunting bad guys, which was far more satisfying.

The two pairs of binocs were expensive, but he didn't care. Liana balked at getting a thick down coat, but he insisted. Along with hats and gloves for the both of them. He used his credit card, not worried about an electronic trail leading out here. They'd be long gone before anyone could find them.

"If you let me drive, you can practice using the binocs," he suggested.

She arched a brow as she'd shrugged into her new coat. "You rarely let me drive when we were together, so don't pretend you're doing me a favor."

He flushed because it was true. "I just want to be sure you're comfortable with them."

"Yeah, sure." She shook her head, looking annoyed, but handed over the keys. "Whatever you say."

"Thanks." It wasn't as if she wasn't a good driver, she was. But he felt better being behind the wheel.

The trip back to the restaurant took another twenty minutes. He drove past the building, glad to see it was still open for business. Whatever role Bai Chow had played was either not critical to the restaurant's day-to-day operations, or he'd already been replaced by someone just as knowledgeable.

And did that general manager job description include participating in the sex-trafficking organization? Maybe.

"Head south here," Liana instructed. "There's a parking place we can use that will give us a view of the kitchen exit."

He did as she suggested. After parking the vehicle in the narrow opening, he shut down the engine and reached for the binocs. "This isn't a great angle," he said, zooming in on the kitchen door. "Not easy to see who is coming or going."

"No, but it's the best we can do. Unless we want to

stand outside in the cold."

It would be cold enough in the car soon, so he didn't complain. They'd used the restrooms in the sporting goods store, so they should be set for a while.

Stakeout duty was the most boring part of a cop's job. And this was no different. He found himself imagining having Lu Chen's for lunch. He never had gotten his takeout order.

He told himself to get over it. They wouldn't starve. Yet the idea of sitting here all day and maybe into the night didn't appeal either.

And they'd have to move the sedan at strategic points throughout the day or risk garnering unwanted attention.

He cracked the car windows to prevent them from fogging up with their breathing and focused on watching the back door. There wasn't much movement in and out of the restaurant, mostly just the occasional kitchen worker tossing a large bag of garbage into the dumpster stationed back there.

When Liana began to shiver, he started the engine.

"I'll be okay," she protested.

"We need to move anyway. Someone will notice if we don't."

"Yeah." She sighed with appreciation as heat poured from the vents. She held her hands up to warm them. "We could watch the front of the restaurant for a while. But most of the staff come in through the back."

"Let's stay with the current plan," he said, driving several blocks out of the way before turning around. "Hopefully, we'll find another parking spot to use."

The next couple of hours passed with excruciating slowness. When his stomach rumbled loud enough for Liana to hear, she took pity on him. "Let's break for lunch.

We should have better luck watching the place at closing time."

"Great." He started the car and pulled out of their fourth parking space. "But I'm in the mood for Chinese."

Her laugh washed over him, making him realize how much he'd missed her. More than he'd admitted even in his darkest days. She patted his knee. "Let's swing by our second favorite restaurant before returning to the hotel."

"I'd like that." He had to remind himself that they were only together now because of the danger due to the way he'd inadvertently blown her cover. And their shared goal of finding Twisted Snake.

But he couldn't deny wanting more. He glanced at her as he drove. After four long months, was getting back together even possible?

Maybe. But he wouldn't tackle that issue yet. Not while gunmen were searching for her. He needed to stay focused on the mission. One wrong move could prove deadly.

For both of them.

Yet he couldn't help testing various scenarios in his mind about how they might find a way to rebuild the foundation of their marriage.

A second chance he wanted more than anything.

LIANA'S NERVES were stretched to the breaking point. She hadn't spent this much time in close quarters with Brock since their honeymoon. Those memories of happier times made it painful to realize how far apart they'd fallen now.

The way he'd accused her of cheating without giving her the benefit of doubt still rankled. Yet she had agreed to do the undercover assignment, which was why Troy was texting her in the first place.

She would never have assumed that a single text from a female meant he was cheating. Yes, she knew Brock had trust issues, but she'd mistakenly thought he'd trusted her. Trusted in their love. In their marriage.

But he hadn't. And here they were, months later, working together in a way they never had before.

Maybe later that day it would be best to split up watching the restaurant from different positions. She didn't think she'd survive another four hours with him in the car.

After grabbing their Chinese to go, Brock returned to the City Central Hotel. She carried their food inside and began unpacking the dozen small, white cardboard boxes.

"I, uh, would like to say grace," Brock said.

She glanced at him in surprise. "You would?"

"Yes." He seemed a little embarrassed as he reached for her hand. "Many of the cops I work with are believers, and I think you and I have a lot to be grateful for."

"Okay." She hadn't grown up attending church, and to her knowledge, Brock hadn't either. She placed her hand in his.

He cleared his throat. "Dear Lord, we thank You for this food we are about to eat. And we ask that You continue to keep us safe in Your care. Amen."

"Amen," she responded. She gently squeezed his fingers before releasing him. "That was nice. You mentioned going to church, but I didn't realize how much you've grown in your faith."

"I'm still fairly new at this," he admitted. "But I have to admit that I have experienced a strange sense of peace while attending services. And praying in general," he added.

This was a side of Brock she'd never seen. It made her wonder if he'd changed in other ways during their time apart.

Their first meeting seemed to indicate he still resented her for taking the assignment. And for leaving, rather than fighting over the fact that she was not having an affair.

"Maybe when this is over, I'll check out that church." She wasn't sure why she'd made the offer, other than it would be a way to stay in touch. Sure, they were getting along now, but she had no illusions that their marriage could be pieced back together so easily.

Brock hadn't trusted her before, and he had less reason to do so now.

Yet the thought of never seeing him again once this was over made her sad. Seeing him in the restaurant had been a shock. She hadn't been happy that he'd blown her cover, yet she had been glad to see him.

Her heart yearned for what they once had. Or at least, what she thought they'd had. Yet if Brock had truly loved her—if he'd really known her the way she thought he did, he wouldn't have jumped to the conclusion she was sleeping with Troy.

Yet that's exactly what he'd done.

"I'd like that," he said softly.

Was he acting like this to make up for the past? Maybe. She concentrated on eating. The food was good, but it was more important to have fuel in their bodies for the rest of the afternoon as they spent more hours watching Lu Chen's. She hoped Dong would know something that could help them. If he didn't? She had no idea what their next steps would be.

Muchin hadn't returned her call. Maybe he'd been surprised to realize she was still alive. The more she thought about the timing of her calling him, then heading to the apartment, the more she believed Muchin had sent Tattoo Guy after her.

"Not as good as Lu Chen's," Brock said. "But I'm not sure I'll ever get food from that restaurant again anyway."

She managed a grim smile. "Yes, I feel the same way. Once I knew what Bai Chow was involved in, I never ate their food again either."

Brock frowned. "Do you think the owner knows?"

"I'm not sure." She sighed. "The owners are a young Chinese couple who took the restaurant over from the young man's parents. It's hard to imagine they're clueless as to what Bai Chow was doing. I assumed they were aware of the link to the Triad."

"Do you have any idea where they live?" Brock asked.

"No. They didn't stop at the restaurant very often either, leaving the day-to-day management to Bai." She straightened. "Although with Bai's death, maybe they would step in. I didn't see either of them entering the kitchen."

"Let's have Rhy do a quick search on their names," Brock suggested.

She hesitated, then nodded. "Okay, fine. Yuze and Lin Lu Chen. Yuze is the oldest male son who took the restaurant over from his father. I don't remember his father's name. I only met them once, and that was months ago."

Brock reached for his phone. "Rhy? I need you to run two names through the system." She listened as he provided the two names, then waited. After a long minute, Brock grimaced and nodded. "Okay, thanks for trying."

"Nothing, right?" she guessed.

"Zip. Not even a parking ticket."

She began clearing up the mess. "We need to head back

to the restaurant. I still think watching the kitchen exit is our best chance of spotting Dong. I don't know that following Yuze and Lin will get us any closer to Twisted Snake. Bai acted as if he were in charge. From what I could tell, the owners were more figureheads than anything. Besides, we know that someone in the kitchen that night, likely Dong or one of the others, may have spoken to Muchin about Bai's arrest. Likely pointing the finger at me, despite my attempt to talk to Muchin first to avoid suspicion."

"You're the expert on this operation," Brock said, surprising her. "Whatever you think is best."

"Thanks." She was surprised he was so amicable. "Let's go, then."

"Can you describe Dong to me?" he asked as they headed back downtown to Lu Chen's restaurant.

"I'll know him when I see him." At his scowl, she quickly added, "Okay, he's about five feet eight inches tall, wears his hair long and tied back in a skinny braid." She pictured Dong in her mind. "He has a narrow face, which is rather striking, and often wears a gold chain around his neck. He also has a small, circular scar under his chin. It's hard to see when facing him but much more noticeable when he looks up."

"Okay, that helps." Brock managed a grim smile. "I just need to get him to look up at the sky."

"Funny." She couldn't help but smile back. She knew that for many people, one Chinese face looked much like the other. Thankfully, Brock was a cop and had a keen eye for detail. Even without the scar, she was fairly certain he'd spot Dong.

They headed back outside into the chilly March wind. She was thrilled with her new coat, a thick downy parka that Brock had insisted on getting at the sporting goods store. It seemed as if she hadn't been warm all winter, between the lack of heat in her apartment and the thin jacket she'd picked up at a secondhand store. The warmth of the coat was incredible.

It was still upsetting to know her undercover assignment was over. And she knew she'd have to reach out to Troy eventually. But not yet.

Not until they had something solid to go on. And she also needed to know she could trust him. Brock's suspicions about her handler had taken root in her mind.

As usual, Brock insisted on driving. She told herself she was better equipped to keep an eye out for trouble anyway.

The restaurant hadn't changed since they'd left two hours ago. When Brock drove past the front of the building, she noticed plenty of diners coming and going, enjoying their mid meal break. As Brock wedged the sedan into a small parking spot that happened to be only fifteen yards from the back door, she settled back into the seat, prepared for another long, boring afternoon.

Stakeouts were not fun.

"When do the kitchen staff take their breaks?" Brock asked.

"Depends on how busy they are." She shrugged. "I remember being in the kitchen midway between lunch and dinner, and half the staff seemed to be missing."

"Some of them live nearby?" Brock asked, scanning the road. "Seems like this area would be too expensive for them."

"I honestly don't know," she admitted. "My job was to meet and exchange information and money with Bai Chow. I only knew Dong because he often stepped in to tell me to wait when Bai wasn't there yet."

"Okay." He drummed his gloved fingers along the top of the steering wheel. "I guess we'll find out sooner or later where Dong lives."

She thought about that. "If we don't spot him in the next couple of hours, we need to come back at closing time. That may be our best chance to follow him home."

"I was afraid of that," he muttered. "It's killing me that we're wasting time out here when we know there are gunmen stalking you."

Those same gunmen wanted to kill Brock, too, but she didn't comment on the obvious. Tattoo Guy likely reported back to Muchin about how she was working with a male partner. If Troy couldn't be trusted, Brock's name and the fact that he was a cop, too, would be easy to uncover.

He'd blown her identity as Feng, and she'd returned the favor by placing him in the line of fire alongside her.

The minutes ticked by slowly. Then she abruptly straightened when an employee came out the back door. Using her binoculars, she zoomed in on the employee.

She needed to see his face to know if he was Dong. He lit a cigarette, then turned to walk away, going around the dumpster.

"Should we follow him?" Brock asked, his binocs trained on the employee too.

"No. I believe he's heading for the bus stop. There's one on the next street." She lowered the glasses, then quickly lifted them again as another employee stepped outside.

"That's Dong," Brock said before she could speak.

"You're right." She kept the glasses focused on Dong. To her surprise, he walked toward them, his head down as he spoke on the phone.

"Get down," Brock said, lowering his head to avoid being seen.

She did so, setting the binocs aside to watch Dong. Thankfully, he was preoccupied with his phone call, but when he strode past, she could hear just a bit of his conversation.

"What's he saying?" Brock asked.

"Something about being there soon." When Dong passed their car, she pushed open her car door. "Let's go."

Brock didn't hesitate. He slid out from behind the wheel and closed the car door as quietly as she did.

She was about to suggest they split up, but Brock came up beside her and looped his arm around her shoulder. He spoke low in her ear. "We're a couple out for a stroll."

"In March?" She huffed as they pretended not to be following Dong. "Seriously?"

"I can help hide your features," Brock insisted. "Dong might recognize you."

That point was difficult to argue, so she dropped the issue. Dong turned right at the next corner. She and Brock quickened their pace to keep up. Her thoughts whirled as they followed him another three blocks to a two-story house that needed a coat of paint but otherwise looked decent.

Who was Dong meeting? Muchin? Maybe they'd decided not to use the restaurant as a meeting location since Bai's arrest.

Dong placed his phone in his pocket and mounted the five steps leading to the front door of the property. The front door opened revealing a large Chinese man. The door closed too quickly for her to get a decent look at him, though.

Muchin? Twisted Snake?

There was only one way to find out, and that was to get inside.

CHAPTER SEVEN

Brock strolled steadily past the house, pretending to be engrossed with Liana. It wasn't difficult. He hadn't held her close in what seemed like years instead of months.

He'd missed her so much.

It wasn't easy to concentrate on the mission when the scent of her hair teased his senses. He wanted her more than he could say.

More than he'd allowed himself to remember.

"We need to get into that house," Liana whispered, breaking into his thoughts.

"Agree, but not until dark," Brock murmured. He tried not to be depressed that she wasn't as affected by their closeness as he was. "Let's walk around the block to check on it from the other side."

She didn't argue, and they continued walking as if they didn't have a care in the world. When they reached the house on the next block that butted up against the backyard of the place Dong had gone, he could see a fence bordering the two properties.

"Darkness is so far away," Liana protested.

"I know, but we can search property records in the meantime. Find out who owns the home."

"That would be great." She looked excited. "This is a good lead, Brock."

"Yeah. It is." He was glad their hours of staking out the restaurant had proven useful. Just when he was ready to pack up and head back to the hotel.

Patience is a virtue, and one he didn't have in abundance. Still, he was glad they'd returned to the restaurant.

As they walked back to Zeke's sedan, still acting their roles of a young couple being in love, he almost tripped when he saw Dong up ahead of them.

"That was a short meeting," Liana whispered, spotting him too. "I wonder what it was about?"

"Should we grab him?" He quickened their pace. "Maybe we can get him to talk."

"Hold on," she protested. "We have the address of the house to dig into. And we know he's heading back to the restaurant. There's no reason to grab him now."

She had a point. Taking Dong to the precinct would potentially tip their hand. Dong himself wasn't as important as whoever was hiring hitmen and running the sex-trafficking organization. And they knew where to find him should things change. "Okay, we'll hold off for now."

Dong didn't seem to notice them as he hurried back to Lu Chen's, moving faster now that he wasn't talking on the phone. Liana was right, the meeting had been short. He imagined Dong had been given orders that were too important to discuss over the phone, before being sent on his way.

By the time they reached Zeke's sedan, Dong was back inside the restaurant. He opened the passenger door for Liana, then ran around to slide in behind the wheel.

He started the engine and cranked the heat. "We need a computer."

She arched a brow. "Does that mean there's another shopping trip on our agenda?"

"Yes." He considered calling one of his teammates—not Steele, who had taken two weeks off to be with his new wife and daughter—but any of the others would drop everything to help him out. Yet he hated dragging them into this. He'd need them soon, but right now, they didn't have much to go on.

"Maybe we should get new smartphones too," Liana said. "I mean, disposable ones are fine, but functionality is severely limited."

He shrugged. "It would be nice, but that would provide an electronic trail leading back to us. I'd rather not do that yet."

"You're right." She grimaced. "We'll make do."

He glanced at her. "It must have been difficult for you to pretend to be someone else, living a completely different lifestyle for the past few months."

She was silent for a long moment. "It's the hardest thing I've ever done," she admitted in a low voice. "I was tempted to quit more times than I care to count."

"Why didn't you?" Even as he asked the question, he knew.

"My cousin Mai Shi." She sighed. "It hurts me to even think about what she's going through."

He nodded, pulling into the parking lot of a big box store. "I'm sorry."

"Me too." She straightened in her seat. "Let's get the computer and return to the hotel. I'm dying to know who owns that house on Duckwood Drive."

The purchase didn't take long. Brock purchased the

simplest and cheapest model they had available. It wasn't like he'd be using it for gaming or graphic design. All they needed was to search public records and maybe social media pages.

When they were back at the City Central Hotel, he quickly plugged it in and pressed the start button. Like Liana, he was anxious to know who owned the property.

"Lakeshore LLC." He scowled. "That's no help."

"A company?" Liana's expression reflected her disappointment. "Can we find out who owns it?"

"I'm not sure I have the tech skills to do that," he said. After several attempts, he pushed the computer aside and reached for his phone. "Gabe, our team's tech guy, should be able to get that information for us."

She placed a hand on his, stopping him. "Are you sure he won't get into trouble for this?"

He considered that for a moment. "I don't think Rhy or Joe will hold it against him. Besides, what other option do we have?" He waved a hand at the computer. "We're no better off now than we were earlier."

"Okay." She reluctantly agreed. "We've come this far."

He punched in Gabe Melrose's number. To his surprise, their tech expert answered right away, despite the unknown number. "Melrose."

"Hey, it's Brock. I need a favor."

"Aren't you on a leave of absence?" Gabe asked. Brock heard keys typing in the background.

"Sort of. But I still need a favor involving your expertise."

"Okay, what is it?" Gabe considered all requests a personal challenge.

"I need to know who owns Lakeshore LLC." He heard Gabe typing the information into his computer. "I tried to look it up on the state website, but I couldn't get any personal information."

"Yeah, they won't let that information hang out there for everyone to see." There was a brief silence. "Hmm. This may take a while."

He tried not to reveal his dismay. "How long? It's important."

"Give me two hours," Gabe said somewhat absently, as if he were already trying to solve the riddle. "I'll call you back."

"Make a note of this number," Brock said. "I'm off-grid."

"Got it." Thankfully, Gabe didn't ask more questions, his attention focused on the issue at hand. "Later."

"Later." He lowered the phone and shrugged at Liana. "He'll do his best."

"Okay, I have another idea anyway." She had tugged the computer toward her. "I entered the address into a map program. This way we can examine it more closely before heading back later tonight."

He leaned forward to peer at the screen. She'd zoomed in on the backyard, which was fenced in. Taking note of the back door and the windows of the basement, he nodded. "Lots of possible entry points."

"Exactly my thought." Her dark eyes gleamed with excitement. "We need a glass cutter to get into the basement. From there, we can make our way up to the main level."

He nodded, even though the idea of getting caught by one or more gunmen didn't appeal. "If you want to do that, we need to wait until midnight."

She frowned, then nodded. "I guess. But if the owners are involved in sex trafficking, they could just as easily be moving girls at that hour."

Looking at the map again, he tapped the tree. "We'll hide here and watch the place for a while before going in. If we see unusual activity, like girls being moved, we'll call for backup and have them arrested."

She frowned. "But what if we don't get Twisted Snake?"

"We'll still have saved several girls. And trust me, we'll find him eventually." He didn't add that he believed there would be several layers of people between Muchin and Twisted Snake. Even arresting Muchin may not lead them to Twisted Snake's real identity.

She was silent for a long moment before she nodded. "Okay. I can live with that. For now."

The last comment bothered him. He held her gaze for a long moment, realizing that no matter what they found later tonight, Liana was not giving up her quest to find Twisted Snake.

A mission that was far more important to her than he was.

BROCK'S green eyes flashed with pain, bringing a fresh wave of guilt. Liana inwardly winced, knowing what he was thinking. He didn't understand how personally important it was for her to bring Twisted Snake to justice.

For her cousin and to honor her mother. She'd loved Brock, or she wouldn't have married him. But this opportunity to work undercover had been too important to ignore.

"I'm sorry." The words were grossly inadequate. She squirmed beneath the intensity of his gaze. "I . . . need a few minutes." She rose and disappeared into one of the bedrooms, closing the door behind her.

Sinking onto the edge of the bed she buried her face in her hands. Hurting Brock was akin to hurting herself. Yet she couldn't afford to give into her weakness. Time to get a grip on her emotions. She needed to stay focused on the end game. Getting inside the property on Duckwood Drive could blow their case wide open.

She desperately wanted to believe they'd find something inside that would lead them to Twisted Snake. Or at the very least to Muchin.

Feeling chilled, she stretched out on the bed, drawing the blanket up to her chin. She envisioned the fenced-in backyard. It would be difficult for anyone to get the girls out through the back, wouldn't it? Unless there was an opening in the fence they weren't aware of.

"Liana?" She opened her eyes to Brock's voice, realizing she'd fallen asleep. "Are you okay?"

"Fine." Her voice was thick with sleep. She cleared her throat, and added, "I'll be right out." She quickly freshened up in the bathroom, then left the bedroom. The enticing scent of spaghetti and meatballs, her favorite, filled the room. "What's this?"

"I ordered room service." He stood off to the side, his hands tucked into the front pockets of his jeans. "I hated to disturb you, but the food was getting cold."

"I didn't mean to conk out like that." She felt silly for sleeping when they had important work to do. "Did you hear from your tech guy?"

"Yeah, he said the LLC is owned by another corporation." He frowned. "Looks like it will take him longer than we thought to peel back the layers. On the bright side, he discovered the restaurant Lu Chen is also owned by the same Lakeshore LLC shell company."

That was interesting. "So maybe the owners of the restaurant are the same owners as the house Dong went to."

"Yes. Or the owners of the restaurant lease the building from the LLC." Brock shrugged. "There's no way to know for sure."

He was right, and it only made her more determined to get to the bottom of this mess. "Maybe we'll find something better once we get inside." She dropped into the closest chair. "Thanks for ordering this, Brock. It looks and smells amazing."

"You're welcome." He took the seat beside her. "If you don't mind, I'd like to say grace again."

"I don't mind." She had to admit this softer side of Brock only made him more attractive.

As if she needed more to like about him. The only thing that had kept her going over these past months without him was the way he'd so readily jumped to the conclusion she was having an affair. She'd convinced herself he hadn't loved her.

Now she had to admit, some of the fault was hers too.

He took her hand, his fingers warm around hers. "Dear Lord Jesus, we thank You for keeping us safe in Your care. We ask that You continue to guide us as we seek the truth and find those young women who need us. Amen."

"Amen." Her voice thickened with emotion. "I hope God does send us to those lost girls. Very soon."

"Me too." His expression was solemn.

The meal was excellent, but thoughts of her cousin Mai Shi had put a damper on her appetite. She knew better than to dwell on the bad stuff. Imagining the worst was crippling. They needed to move forward. To find these girls as soon as humanly possible.

No matter the cost to them personally.

A quick glance at the microwave revealed it was later than she'd anticipated. "I can't believe it's quarter past eight o'clock at night."

"You slept for several hours, which is a good thing." Brock smiled crookedly. "Sleep hasn't been a luxury lately."

"For you either."

He shrugged. "I managed to sleep for an hour."

They ate in silence for several minutes. But for once it was a comfortable silence. Some of their earlier awkwardness had faded. Giving her hope that maybe, just maybe, they'd find a way to reunite when this was over.

She wasn't sure their marriage could be saved, yet she hoped they could remain on friendly terms.

When they'd finished eating, Brock set the tray of dirty dishes outside their room. "I was thinking we should leave soon. We need to get the glass cutters for one thing, and the hardware store closes at nine. After that, I thought it would be best to get in position under the tree earlier than later."

"I am in total agreement." She was eager to get back to the property. "Let's hit the road."

They shrugged into their coats and left the suite, using the side door to exit the building. Outside, the night sky was dark, a low cloud shelf blocking any potential light from the moon and the stars. The city lights were still bright enough to see at least a few feet in front of her, and that would have to be good enough.

The trip to the hardware store took longer than she'd expected. Brock left with more than just a glass cutter; he'd purchased several screwdrivers, plastic ties, two thin flashlights, and a box cutter. She was surprised when he handed her the box cutter along with one of the flashlights.

"I have a knife." He pocketed the screwdrivers, plastic ties, flashlight, and glass cutter. "Ready?"

She didn't ask why they'd need knives when they had guns. Cops generally had more than one weapon at their disposal. Every situation was different, and it was always best to be prepared. "Yes. Let's do this."

The ride to Duckwood Drive didn't take too long. Brock spent another ten minutes searching for a place to park. He finally found a spot four blocks away.

This time, he didn't pretend to be enamored of her. They simply walked side by side, both sweeping their gazes over the area.

Brock led the way to the back side of the property. There were lights on in the house that butted up against their target, but he didn't hesitate to lead the way through the backyard to the fence.

He climbed over it first, and she quickly followed, landing on the hard ground on the other side with a soft thud. Brock drew her toward the large tree. There weren't any leaves on the branches this time of the year, but the trunk was wide enough to offer some protection. Their dark clothing helped too.

She crouched behind the tree, gazing intently at the house. "No lights," she whispered.

"I noticed." Brock frowned. "Could be there's no one inside."

They were quiet for a solid ten minutes. There was no sign of life inside the place, and she didn't hear anything either. Sweeping her gaze over the structure, she didn't find a single camera or motion sensor lights.

Maybe the activity there was such they didn't want cameras or lights.

As the minutes ticked by, she felt certain they wouldn't have to wait until midnight. If there was no sign of anyone being there, they could go ahead with the plan.

Yet she couldn't help feeling let down by the apparent lack of activity inside. She'd really hoped they'd find some of the girls. Or even Muchin himself.

They needed to find some evidence of the sex-trafficking operation. If this location didn't pan out, they'd have little choice but to get a search warrant for the restaurant, the way Brock had suggested. Even though that would likely send Muchin and Twisted Snake into hiding.

After another long ten minutes, Brock finally leaned close. "Let's enter through the basement window."

She nodded in relief. He pulled out the glass cutter and darted across the yard. She followed close behind.

As he worked on the glass, she turned to watch their backs. There was nothing but an eerie silence from the closest neighbors.

The sound of glass cutting seemed extraordinarily loud to her ears. But no lights flicked on from inside. And she didn't notice any curtains moving as if by someone looking out.

Somehow, Brock managed to remove the glass without making a mess. He set the glass pane aside and then rocked back onto his heels. "You're smaller, so I'll need you to go first. I may not be able to get through."

"I understand." If he couldn't fit his broad shoulders through the window, she'd have to open a door for him. She poked her head through the opening, checking the space below. This window happened to be in front of the wash basin. Turning so she could put her feet through the opening first, she lowered herself through the window.

Her toes found the edge of the wash tub, holding her steady as she shimmied through the opening. Silently praying the tub would hold her weight, she placed both feet on the edge, then turned and hopped down.

Turning on her flashlight, she examined the space. Spying a small step stool, she brought it over for Brock. His weight might be too much for the wash basin.

He came through feet first, too, but then had to do some twisty maneuvers to get his shoulders through.

It worked. Five minutes later, they were making their way through the basement.

They didn't talk as they performed a quick search of the basement. The walls on one side were damp, a small puddle of water forming in the corner. There were boxes and boxes piled up against another wall, but there wasn't time to go through them now. Besides, a thin layer of dust covered them, indicating they hadn't been packed recently.

She gestured to the stairs leading up to the main floor. Brock nodded, his expression grim. He shut off his flashlight, and she did the same before placing her weight on the first step.

The wood creaked loudly, like an old lady groaning in pain.

She froze, her pulse spiking with fear. But after several long moments, she took the next step. And the next.

Several of the stairs creaked, but stepping closer to one side or the other minimized the sound. The door at the top of the stairs was closed. She reached for the handle, hoping it wasn't locked.

The handle turned beneath her fingers. She opened the door just a crack, trying to stay positioned to one side in case there was someone standing there, waiting to shoot.

Brock managed to move up the stairs more quietly than she had. He positioned himself on the other side, giving her a nod to indicate he was ready.

She pushed the door all the way open while staying back.

Nothing.

Stepping up onto the landing, she found herself in a small alcove between the kitchen and living room. She headed into the kitchen and dining room, leaving Brock to clear the living room and half bathroom. She found it interesting there was no sign of anyone living there. No newspapers, magazines, or books. No plants or family photographs.

There were a few coasters on the end tables but no empty glasses or other dishes lying around. The entire house smelled stale and musty, and if she hadn't watched a large Chinese man open the door for Dong, she'd have assumed the place had remained empty for the past several months.

After a brief yet thorough search, she met up with Brock near the basement door. They exchanged a look, sharing a sense of frustration at not finding anything helpful.

Could the occupants be upstairs, sleeping? It wasn't that late, but anything was possible.

She gestured toward the steps leading to the second floor. Brock nodded and fell into step behind her.

These steps were carpeted, and she tried to step toward the edges to avoid more creaking. The second step to the top groaned loudly, causing her to freeze in place again. But as before, she didn't see or hear anyone coming to investigate.

At the top of the stairs, she found a hallway with several doors on each side. She pointed to the left, while Brock stepped to the right.

Each of the bedrooms was empty. And only one of them, the master suite, had bedding that looked relatively fresh. Maybe Yuze and Lin Lu Chen, the restaurant owners, did spend some time here. But she was sure the large Chinese man who'd opened the door for Dong wasn't Yuze. The owner was a much shorter and thinner man.

"Now what?" she asked in a whisper as they returned to the main floor. "Dong came here for a reason."

Brock slowly shook his head. "I feel like we're missing something."

"Yeah, a clue." She couldn't help sounding dejected. "I really thought we'd find some sort of evidence. It doesn't even look like the bedrooms upstairs are being used, except for the master."

"And the bathroom medicine cabinet and vanity drawers are empty." He seemed equally depressed. "Let's check the basement again."

"Why not? We may as well go out the same way we came in," she said on a sigh.

"Did you notice that wood paneling?" Brock asked as he headed down the basement stairs. She followed, taking a moment to close the basement door behind her.

"The one near the stack of boxes?" She met him at the bottom of the stairs.

"Yes." Brock walked toward it, playing his light along the fake wood paneling. "Check this out."

It was a very thin, barely able to be seen door hinge. Two of them.

Brock ran his fingers along the other side of the paneling, then dug his fingernails into a groove and pulled. She gasped when a door opened revealing another set of stairs. These were made of rough cement.

She stepped forward, intending to find out where they led, when Brock abruptly stopped her.

And that's when she heard muted voices. There were at least two people on the other end of the cement stairs. People who could very well be coming toward them.

CHAPTER EIGHT

Brock wanted to get Liana out of there as soon as humanly possible. They needed more information before barging through the tunnel. But, of course, she shook off his hand to creep up the stairs.

Gritting his teeth, he followed. This house must connect via this secret staircase to the property next door. That house, he remembered, had lights blazing from the windows. And he'd wished he'd checked to see if the owner of the property was also Lakeshore LLC.

Liana moved slowly and thankfully stopped at the halfway point. He realized the voices were clearer now. Except for the part where they spoke in rapid Chinese.

After a long moment, Liana turned to glance at him. She looked like she wanted to say something but didn't. Instead, she gestured for them to return to the basement.

When they were back in the basement, she closed the door, then moved to the other side of the room. "I think Muchin is in there. I heard three distinct voices."

"What were they saying?"

"Nothing specific to sex trafficking or Twisted Snake,

but they did discuss the need to eliminate the threat." She pointed to him, then to herself. "You and me."

That wasn't necessarily a surprise. "Did they use our real names?"

"No, they simply referred to us as two thorns stuck in their sides." She gestured to the hidden door. "Do you think we can get a search warrant?"

It was a good question. They didn't have evidence of sex trafficking, but Liana had heard Muchin's voice. "I'll talk to Rhy. In the meantime, we need to get out of here."

She frowned without moving. "I'll stay here and keep listening. You go outside and talk to Rhy. We know the men are there now. If we wait, we could lose them."

"I'm not leaving you here." He scowled. "We may not have enough for a search warrant. And if that's the case, we'll need to keep an eye on the place to get what we need. If we can get a photo of Muchin going in or out, or girls being moved in and out, then we'll get the entire tactical team to breach the place."

She was about to protest when the sound of voices grew louder.

They were coming closer!

Liana met his gaze, and in silent agreement, they both ran toward the open basement window. He would have preferred not to leave evidence behind, like an open window that had been expertly cut away, but it couldn't be helped. He waited for Liana to crawl up through the opening first, then he used the step stool to follow. In his haste, his shoulders got stuck. He wiggled around and managed to get one arm through, then the other. Liana helped pull him through.

The voices were louder now. Whoever was coming

through the connection between the two buildings was almost in the basement.

Despite knowing it wouldn't help much, he propped the removed glass up against the opening. Then they dashed back to the fence. He gave Liana a leg up, practically vaulting her over, then quickly scaled it for himself, half expecting to be used as target practice.

But all was quiet.

They darted through the neighboring yard, then reached the street. When he glanced back over his shoulder, he saw the glow of light coming from the kitchen. He stopped, reaching for the binocs, but the fence was too high, impeding his line of sight.

"Let's head around the block and watch from the front," Liana whispered.

He nodded. They moved swiftly, and he worried that the minute they noticed the cold air coming in through the basement window, the men speaking Chinese would bolt out of there.

Liana sprinted up ahead, reaching the corner first. He considered heading for Zeke's sedan, then dismissed the idea. When they'd driven past the property earlier, there hadn't been any open parking spots.

Better for them to stay on foot.

When they rounded the corner of Duckwood Drive, Liana darted across the street, using the vehicles parked there for cover. He quickly joined her, dropping behind an SUV. He let out a sigh of relief to see that there was a light on in the kitchen of the property they'd just escaped from. They must not have noticed the open window.

And lights glowed in the property to the south too. That meant some of the voices they'd heard had stayed put, while others had crossed to the adjacent property. He couldn't believe the two houses were connected by a secret stairwell. The houses were built years ago, so maybe the passage was from the old bootlegging days?

Liana had her binocs trained on the kitchen window of the house they'd left. He focused his lenses on the house to the south. But he still couldn't see anyone moving inside. A moment later, the lights went off.

The front door opened. He moved his binocs to get a closer look. A large Chinese man stepped outside. The size of the guy was similar to the one who'd opened the door earlier to let Dong in.

Could this man be Twisted Snake? Or Muchin? He watched the large man move but couldn't see any tattoos.

The Chinese man strode toward them. Belatedly realizing the SUV must belong to him, he lowered the binocs and tugged Liana's arm. They crawled to the next car, using the vehicle for coverage. Thankfully, the large Chinese man didn't seem to notice, he simply got in behind the wheel and started the engine.

When the vehicle headed down the road, he memorized the license plate, make, and model of the SUV. Liana had her binocs zoomed in on the kitchen window. When that light went out, too, he decided it was time to move.

"Let's go." There was no way to know which of the parked cars might belong to the occupant in the house.

The front door opened, and this time, two Chinese men stepped out. One was Dong; the other he had never seen before. He followed Liana to the next parked car and the next. But unlike the first guy, these two men turned and walked in the opposite direction.

"They may be going back to the restaurant," Liana whispered.

He thought that was highly likely. "Let's get to the sedan. We should be able to catch up with them there."

She nodded. After the two men turned the corner, she rose and ran down the block. He kept pace behind her. He was glad they were getting closer to uncovering the truth. The connection between the two houses, the two men returning to the restaurant, and having the large Chinese man's license plate number.

He was confident they'd get a search warrant by morning.

They reached Zeke's sedan in record time. He drove directly to the restaurant, searching for the two men who'd left the house.

But there was no sign of them.

"Where are they?" He glanced at Liana. "Maybe they weren't heading back to the restaurant."

She frowned. "I recognized them as kitchen workers. Dong, obviously, but I don't know the name of the other guy."

"So the big Chinese man wasn't Muchin," he said.

"No." She sighed. "I must have been mistaken about hearing his voice. Maybe one of them was Twisted Snake, although I wouldn't expect him to meet directly with a lower-level employee like Dong. I'm wondering if the big Chinese man could be replacing Bai Chow."

He nodded thoughtfully. "It seems as if they didn't notice the window." He glanced at her as they approached the restaurant. "I think we should head back and repair it."

Lu Chen's was completely dark. If Dong and his buddy had returned, they were sitting inside without any lights on. Highly unlikely. He drove past the restaurant. "We need caulk or something to use on the window." He wished he'd have thought of that while at the hardware store. It was closed now, so any repairs would have to wait until morning.

"I think we should go back and get into the second house. Maybe there's something there that will help us."

He shook his head. "Doubtful. They're too smart for that. These homes are just meeting places. Maybe someone sleeps there on occasion, but tonight, everyone left. Three voices, three men. I need to call Gabe about the license plate. That's our best lead right now."

She was quiet for a long moment. "Okay, we'll tackle the license plate first. But I was hoping we'd know more. Other than discovering the secret connection between the two properties, we didn't get much."

"That's true, but every little bit counts." He turned around to head back to the City Central Hotel. He'd call Grayson to repair the window. Getting a search warrant for the two properties wouldn't help if there weren't girls being held against their will. They needed to find a way to link the men they'd seen tonight to the sex-trafficking organization.

Pressing charges was useless without proof.

"I wonder if your tech buddy could find other properties owned by Lakeshore LLC," Liana said. "Maybe we can check them out too. The girls must be going somewhere."

"Good point." He pulled up near the side exit of the City Central Hotel. He didn't head inside but called Gabe first.

"Do you know what time it is?" Gabe Melrose demanded. "I'm off duty."

"I know. I'm sorry. But I need another favor. Just a quick license plate run," he added. "Then I'll leave you alone until tomorrow."

"I'm off duty," Gabe repeated. Then he sighed. "Fine. Give me the plate number."

Brock rattled it off. He heard keys tapping, knowing full well Gabe was always near a computer.

"Yeah, okay, it belongs to a guy named Yuze Lu Chen," Gabe said. "Does that mean anything to you?"

He met Liana's gaze with a surge of satisfaction. "It does, yes. Thanks, Gabe. Tomorrow, I'd like a list of all known properties belonging to Lakeshore LLC."

"Tomorrow," Gabe repeated. "I'm beat."

"Understood, thanks." He lowered the phone. "Looks like that's another connection to the restaurant. I doubt Yuze would give his SUV to a stranger."

"They are involved in the criminal side of this," Liana murmured, her brow furrowed. "I had hoped they weren't."

He understood her concern. The owners were neck-deep in trafficking young women, not figureheads as she'd believed.

He hoped that by morning the list of properties owned by Lakeshore LLC would give them something more to go on.

They needed to shut down this sex-trafficking organization, once and for all.

BACK IN THE HOTEL ROOM, Liana bid Brock good night, heading into her room. Physically, she was exhausted, but her mind wouldn't stop spinning over the various possibilities of the large Chinese man's identity.

Was she wrong about him not being Twisted Snake? And where was Muchin? She'd expected to see him there tonight. She understood that Dong and his cohort must have been promoted up the ranks. Did that mean Muchin was higher in the organization now too?

Obviously, he wasn't going to return her call, much less set up a meeting. And since she had no idea where he lived, there was no way to find him.

This entire operation was starting to feel like a big fat failure. For all she knew, Twisted Snake had left the area. He could be in another city and state, or even all the way back in China.

Despair washed over her. She thought about how Brock had begun attending church and the way he'd prayed for God to keep them safe.

Why hadn't God kept her cousin Mai Shi safe?

She squeezed her eyes shut against a spurt of hot tears, wishing more than anything she had found her cousin tonight. Or any of the girls who'd been taken by Muchin and Twisted Snake. It wasn't right that so many should suffer at their hands.

Be still and know that I am God.

The words flashed in her mind, and the tiny hairs lifted along her arms. Was that a verse from the Bible? She felt certain it was, but she'd never read the Bible.

Oddly, a sense of peace washed over her. She rolled off the bed and opened the door, peering into the main living space. She'd left Brock on the phone with Grayson, asking him to repair the window they'd cut from the frame.

The room was empty, and Brock's bedroom door was closed.

She'd thought maybe he'd said the words out loud, but that obviously wasn't the case. Besides, she hadn't heard the words as if they were spoken out loud, but rather had experienced them, deep inside her mind.

Which didn't make any sense.

She sighed, raking her hand through her hair. The stress

of working this operation with Brock was getting to her. She needed sleep.

After a long moment, she returned to her room.

A few hours later, she awoke with a start, her heart pounding. Was that a noise? Or her imagination?

She struggled to control her breathing, listening intently. But when there was nothing but silence, she relaxed.

Her imagination was working overtime tonight.

Now that she was awake, though, she couldn't seem to fall back asleep. She finally crawled out of bed and washed up in the bathroom. The hour was early, barely five thirty in the morning, so coffee was a necessity.

Peeking into the main suite, she noticed it was still empty. Brock's door remained closed too. Crossing to the kitchenette, she quickly filled the coffeemaker with water and added the package of grounds provided by the hotel.

When the coffee was ready, she carried her mug to the sofa. She was anxious to get back to work. How early would Brock's tech guy get into the precinct? They needed that list of properties. The girls must be stashed somewhere close by.

She wanted to believe that today was the day they'd find them.

Sipping her coffee, she decided to give Brock thirty minutes. The poor guy needed sleep, but the girls needed to be found too.

Less than ten minutes later, Brock emerged from the bedroom, his hair damp from a recent shower. For a second, it was as if they were back at the condo. She almost rose from the sofa to greet him with a kiss but managed to hold herself back.

If she kissed him, she might never stop.

"Good morning." His low voice sent tingles of awareness down her spine.

"Good morning." She strove to sound unaffected by his nearness. "I made coffee."

"Thanks." He crossed over to pour himself some. He glanced at her over his shoulder. "Before you ask, I texted Gabe. No response yet."

"You read my mind," she said with a smile.

"Not always." His brow furrowed. "I know I hurt you."

His lack of trust had hurt. But she wasn't innocent in this. "Yes, but I hurt you too."

Brock crossed over to sit beside her. "Liana, when this is over—" He stopped when his phone chimed with an incoming text.

"Is that Gabe?" She leaned closer, trying to read the screen.

"Yes." He set his coffee aside to text back, both thumbs working the screen. "He's heading into work. He'll have something for us soon."

"That's good to hear." She sighed. "I don't want to sit here doing nothing."

He nodded. After sending the text, he picked up his coffee. "We should order breakfast. It may take time to get through the list of properties."

"Okay." She wanted to ask him what he was about to say. When this was over, what? Did he want a second chance?

Did she?

Yes.

But not if things just went back to the way they were.

The conversation they needed to have hung in the air between them. But the words remained unspoken.

Why was this so difficult?

"Should I order the usual?" Brock asked.

She belatedly realized he was standing near the table, holding the menu. "That sounds good."

After he placed the order, his phone chimed again. This time the text was from Grayson.

Brock scooped up his phone. "The window is repaired," he said. He looked up from the screen. "Grayson and Raelyn checked the place out first, but it was empty."

"It seems like such a waste to have two houses that aren't being used except for meetings." She shook her head. "I feel like we're missing something."

"I had that same thought." He frowned, texting back. "Hopefully the other properties will reveal more information."

"They better." She didn't think they were wrong about Lakeshore LLC being tied to the sex-trafficking operation.

"Rhy wants to chat." He grimaced. "With both of us."

That didn't sound reassuring either. Brock made the call and placed the phone on speaker.

"Brock? You have Liana there too?" Rhy asked.

"I'm here," she said. "What's the problem?"

"Lieutenant Troy Wallace set up a meeting with me." Rhy didn't beat around the bush. "He's asking about the two of you."

"Don't trust him," Brock warned. "He's likely the reason Liana's cover was blown."

"Really?" Rhy's tone was dry. "I thought you were the one who did that."

"I did," Brock agreed. "But gunmen have been tracking her ever since, even to locations they shouldn't know anything about." He met her gaze. "Like the family restaurant where Troy was supposedly bringing a backup vehicle for her to use. Only a gunman showed up instead."

"Yes, I know. I had to do a lot of talking to get you off the hook on that incident, remember?" Rhy sounded testy. "Wallace is still a cop. And he wants information related to an operation he spent a lot of time and tax-dollar money funding."

"Tell him we're still working the case," she said. "But without his help."

There was a long pause. "Not sure that will go over very well," Rhy finally said. "Keep in mind you're both working this case on your own, without official support from the MPD. That's generally a recipe for disaster."

"Maybe, but it's our only option," Brock interjected. "We've been safe here for the past twenty-four hours, since we evaded the gunman at the restaurant. I'd like to keep it that way. I have Gabe working on some information that could blow the case wide open. If Troy wants credit, he'll have to wait for us to get the proof we need."

"I don't think this is about getting credit," Rhy said calmly. "I think he's concerned about Liana's safety."

"I'm safe with Brock," she said. "And we're making some progress." Not a lot, but she worked hard to sound confident. "Let Troy know we're doing our best to uncover the identity of the man known as Twisted Snake."

Another long pause. "Okay, I know what it's like to be in a situation like yours. I'll smooth things over with Wallace."

"We appreciate that, Rhy." Brock looked relieved. "We need to continue flying under the radar as much as possible. He should understand that."

"Keep me informed," Rhy said. "I don't want to lose two good cops, understand?"

She couldn't help exchanging a smile with Brock. He

said, "Thanks, Rhy. I plan on bringing the team in if we find something."

"Troy's here now. We'll talk later." Rhy disconnected from the call.

"I thought you were going to ask for a search warrant for the restaurant?" she asked.

"I thought about it, but other than three properties all owned by Lakeshore LLC, we don't have any evidence of wrongdoing." He shrugged. "Yes, Bai worked there, was arrested and murdered, but that doesn't mean the entire restaurant is involved. And as you pointed out, if there was evidence there, it was probably moved."

She sighed. "We need to connect the restaurant to criminal activity."

"Exactly." A knock at the door interrupted him. Brock jumped up and went to the door, checking the peephole before opening it. "Thanks." He tipped the guy and set the tray on the table.

She rose to join him. He gestured to the seat beside him. "I'd like to say grace."

"That sounds nice." She thought again of the words that had gone through her mind. *Be still and know that I am God.*

"Dear Lord Jesus, we thank You for this food we are about to eat. We ask that You keep us safe and that You guide us on the right path to save those who are in danger. Amen."

"Amen." She sat for a moment, then dug into her food. The sooner they finished, the sooner they could head out to the Lakeshore LLC properties Gabe was pulling together for them.

As if reading her mind, Brock's phone dinged. "This is Gabe now. He has five properties for us to look at."

"Five aside from the two on Duckwood Drive and the restaurant?" She was surprised. "That's great. Where should we start?"

Brock munched a strip of bacon as he scrolled through the text. "Not two on Duckwood. Interestingly, the house to the south isn't owned by Lakeshore LLC. It's under the name of David Kimball."

She frowned. "Who is that?"

"No clue. But Gabe is going to look for more places owned by Kimball too."

This could take longer than she'd anticipated. How many people were a part of this organization anyway? And why an American sounding name rather than a Chinese one?

"What about the others?"

He nodded slowly. "Most look to be single-family homes, except for one." He grimaced. "A motel by the name of Lake View Motel. It's about five miles north from Lu Chen's."

Her stomach tightened at the implication. "That's our first stop."

Brock's serious gaze met hers. "Agree."

She found herself eating even faster now, anxious to hit the road. Brock, too, finished his breakfast in record time. After taking a quick bathroom break, she shrugged into her new coat. Brock tucked their new computer under his arm before leading the way out of the hotel suite.

He turned to the left toward the side exit. Pausing, he glanced around, then pushed through the door. Since he had the keys and always wanted to drive, she headed for the passenger seat without complaint.

Brock opened the back seat of the sedan and tossed the computer in.

She was about to open her door when movement caught the corner of her eye. She whirled, her hand reaching for her weapon. Something sailed past her head, landing in the center of the passenger seat. It was shaped like a canister.

"Down!" Brock shouted, seconds before the canister exploded.

CHAPTER NINE

Brock was momentarily blinded by the flash, his ears ringing from the explosion. Yet he didn't feel any pain. Picking himself off the ground, he blinked, trying to see what was happening.

"Liana?" Fear gripped him tightly around the throat. "Liana? Are you okay?"

He couldn't hear her response but wasn't sure if that was because of the ringing in his ears. Running his hands over his body, he didn't find any injuries.

The explosion must have been a flash-bang. Enough to cause temporary blindness and deafness.

Feeling his way along the vehicle, he squinted, trying to see. "Liana!"

"Let me go!" A hoarse voice reached his ears.

Understanding the flash-bang had been a diversion to grab Liana, he surged forward, arms wide, hoping to run into Liana and the assailant. Unable to see, he tried to focus on the sounds of the struggle.

The tip of his right hand brushed someone. He quickly

spun in that direction. He plowed directly into two struggling bodies.

"Oomph." He couldn't tell who had made the sound.

"Liana!" A fist connected with his jaw, snapping his head back. Pain exploded in his head. Ignoring it, he blinked, seeing the vague shadows of two figures still struggling. One much smaller.

He charged toward them, aiming at the larger figure. Somehow, he managed to catch the assailant off guard, and the figures broke apart. But then he was hit again in the center of his chest with enough force to send him staggering backward.

"Brock!" Liana's cry came through louder now. He focused on the larger man, who appeared to be taking off, giving up the fight.

"Grab him!" He lurched toward him, desperate to get the suspect into custody.

Liana darted forward, but it was too late. From somewhere outside his line of vision, he heard a car door slamming shut and the roar of an engine as the assailant got away.

Liana bent over, holding one arm against her chest.

"You're hurt?" He quickly joined her, placing his arm around her shoulder. "What happened?"

"He twisted my wrist." She winced. "I hope it's not broken."

A red haze of fury clouded his vision. He struggled to remain calm. "We need to get out of here. They know our location."

"I know." She blinked at him. "That was a flash-bang, right? I initially thought it was a hand grenade."

"Me too." Ignoring his own aches and pains, he urged her forward. "Let's go."

The flash-bang had deployed in the front passenger seat, leaving a chemical mess of magnesium, copper, and other debris behind. No broken windows, thankfully. They needed to get a few miles away from the hotel before abandoning the vehicle.

And he'd owe Zeke for the repairs.

Liana climbed into the back while he took the wheel. He drove out of the parking lot and headed downtown. Rather than abandon the car where it would be towed, he found a surface parking lot and paid for a week.

Hopefully enough time for them to retrieve the sedan.

"Should we bring the laptop?" Liana asked.

"Yes." He took the computer case from her. "Thanks."

"I wonder why he tried to grab me rather than outright killing me." Liana took his hand, much the way she used to, as they walked away from the parking lot.

He grimaced, his head throbbing. "I'm sure they planned to force you into the sex-trafficking trade."

She shivered. He tugged her closer, wishing there was time to rest and relax. "I'm okay," she whispered.

"God was watching over us, Liana," he said. "It's a good thing the assailant didn't just shoot you. His plan failed."

"I know." She sighed, her fingers tightening on hers. "But he escaped."

He wasn't happy about that either, but they were alive, and that was the most important thing. "How's your arm?"

"Hurts." She'd tucked her left hand into her coat pocket. "Where are we headed?

"To the courthouse, well actually, the administrative building nearby."

"What? Why?"

"I've met ADA Bax Scala a few times when I was needed to testify in court. Bax is married to Kyleigh Scala,

Rhy's sister. I'm hoping I can use his phone to call Rhy. After the way we were found at the hotel, I don't want to use our cell phones. And we need access to another vehicle." He glanced at her. "Once we have a new ride, we'll get you to the hospital for X-rays."

"No need. I'm fine."

"You can't ignore a possible broken wrist." He tried to keep his voice even. "It won't take too long."

"I'm fine," she repeated testily. "We'll stop and grab a wrist brace and a cold pack. Even if the bone is broken, they can't do much until the swelling goes down."

"You're a medical expert now?"

"I twisted my ankle in high school, and that was verbatim what the doctor told me. This is much the same sort of injury." She sighed. "Besides, we don't have time. We need to check out the Lake View Motel."

He shared her concern about the motel. Was she right about the swelling? It made sense. But he still wanted her wrist examined by a doctor.

When they passed a corner drug store, he tugged on her hand. "Let's get those supplies now."

She didn't argue. He wove through the aisles, quickly finding what they needed. A sling, a wrap, and a cold pack. After a moment's hesitation, he added a bottle of ibuprofen and two bottles of water.

He led the way to the bus stop bench just outside the building. When he saw the dark bruises already forming on her wrist, he winced. "Liana. That looks so painful."

"I'll survive."

He drew her close, wishing more than anything she'd never taken this undercover assignment. But she was a cop, and injuries were always a risk of the job. He'd never ask her to give up her career. Especially one she loved.

Liana leaned against him for a moment. He pressed a kiss to her temple. She glanced up in surprise. His gaze dropped to her mouth.

He kissed her, gently at first, then deepening the kiss as if the months they'd spent apart hadn't happened.

A large bus lumbered toward them. He broke off the kiss, realizing this wasn't the place or the time.

The doors of the bus opened, and several people got out. Ignoring them, he helped her take her coat off. First, he wrapped her wrist loosely in the elastic bandage, then placed the arm sling over her shoulder. He cracked the cold pack and tucked it against her injured wrist. "Can you hold that close to your body?"

"Yes." She repositioned it to a more comfortable position. "Thanks."

"Lastly, we're both taking these." He opened the ibuprofen and shook four tablets into his palm. She downed hers first, then he took some too. As they sipped their water, the bus rolled off.

"Ready?" he asked.

She nodded, lifting her head to meet his gaze. "Thanks, Brock."

He wanted to kiss her again but forced himself to stand. Even after all this time, he still wanted her. Only her.

No one else.

And he wasn't sure how or if they'd find their way back together again.

LIANA'S PULSE didn't settle back down for long minutes after Brock's incredible kiss. If not for the stupid bus showing up, they'd still be kissing.

She wanted nothing more than to kiss him again, yet that seemed wrong when they had work to do.

She and Brock reached the administrative building five minutes later. He stepped up to address the receptionist. Normally, Steele's fiancée, Harper, would be sitting there, but she was out on maternity leave. This woman was likely a temp. "ADA Bax Scala, please. Let him know Brock Greer, one of Rhy's tactical team members, needs a moment of his time."

The woman made the call, then motioned toward the door. "Go ahead. His office is down the hall on the left."

"Thank you." He drew Liana with him. The door to Bax's office was open, and the ADA looked up in surprise when they stepped inside.

"ADA Scala? I'm Brock Greer. And this is, uh"—he stumbled a bit over the introduction—"Liana."

Had he been about to introduce her as his wife? She told herself it didn't matter.

"Come on in," Bax said with a smile. The guy wore a pricey suit and glanced at what appeared to be an expensive watch. "I have fifteen minutes before I need to head over to the courthouse."

"We won't keep you, and I'm sorry to barge in like this," Brock said. "We'd like to borrow your landline phone to make a brief call. I—we're in danger, and I need to contact Rhy about obtaining a replacement vehicle."

"The Finnegans spent an entire year going through cars as if replacements came in small boxes from the toy store." Bax shook his head with a sigh. "No reason to call Rhy. I'm happy to arrange a car for you to use."

"Oh, we couldn't possibly accept that," Liana interjected. She hoped Bax didn't think they had come to take advantage of the connection between him and Rhy.

"I insist." Bax picked up his phone. "This will only take a minute. Have a seat. You look as if you've been in a fight or something."

"Or something," Brock murmured. He exchanged a glance with Liana as they sank into the pair of chairs facing Bax's desk. He looked as taken aback by the ADA's offer as she was. "I'm happy to reimburse you," Brock added.

"Not necessary." Bax flashed a warm smile, then turned his attention to the phone. "This is Baxter Scala. I need a car delivered to the courthouse as soon as possible."

Delivered? Liana tried to hide her shock. She could only imagine how much that would cost.

"Thanks." Bax replaced the phone. "All set."

"That's very generous," Liana managed. "But we really only came to use your phone."

"I know, but I truly don't mind." Bax shrugged. "I'm always willing to donate for a good cause. And there's nothing more important than helping my wife's brothers and sisters in blue."

"I—thank you," Brock said.

"Yes, thank you. We're very grateful," Liana added.

Bax stood. "Is there anything else you need? Cash?"

"No, thanks." From the look in Brock's eye, she could tell he was drawing the line at taking the ADA's cash. ADAs didn't make that much money, but Bax acted like he had plenty to spare. Based on the suit and watch, maybe he did.

"Ah, we should head over to the courthouse now," she said. "We don't want to make you late for court."

"Yeah, most judges frown on tardiness," Bax agreed. The lawyer took a moment to shove files into his briefcase, along with a laptop computer. She was glad she'd remembered to pull theirs from the back seat. It would come in handy in locating the properties owned by Lakeshore LLC.

"This way," Bax said, leading the way through the narrow offices. She noticed some of the younger lawyers only had cubicles but that both Bax Scala and Maddy Sinclair had their own private offices.

"You're sure there isn't anything else you need?" Bax asked as they stepped into the cold. "I truly don't mind."

"The car is more than enough," Brock insisted. She wondered if he was concerned about what Rhy would think about using the connection to Bax Scala.

"Do you have a big case you're working on?" she asked.

"Just a motion hearing on a carjacking case," Bax admitted. "I expect the defense lawyer is going to accept a plea deal."

She wanted to ask if Bax was aware of any sex-trafficking cases but decided against it. That information wouldn't necessarily help them find Muchin, the large Chinese man, Twisted Snake, or any of the other members of the sex-trafficking ring.

And that needed to be their focus. She wasn't going to worry about her injured arm when those girls experienced so much worse.

She hoped that when—not if—they broke the organization wide open, that Bax Scala or Maddy Sinclair would be the prosecutors assigned to the case.

She wouldn't be satisfied until those involved in trafficking girls spent the rest of their miserable lives behind bars.

"What happened to your arm?" Bax asked.

"I sprained my wrist," Liana explained, downplaying the injury.

"Looks like it hurts." Bax frowned. "You should get that looked at by a doctor."

She nodded. "Soon."

Brock arched a brow, letting her know he'd hold her to that.

Upon reaching the front of the courthouse, Bax scanned the street. "I think that's your car," he said, nodding toward a shiny black SUV.

"Thanks again." Brock held out his hand. Bax shook it. "We owe you for this."

"Never, no strings. But please take care of yourselves." Bax frowned, glancing at Liana's injured arm again. "Stay safe."

"Always the goal," Brock agreed.

"We appreciate everything you've done for us," she echoed Brock's gratitude.

The driver slid out from behind the wheel of the SUV. He tossed the key fob to Bax, who handed it to Brock. Then he tipped the guy.

"Thanks, Mr. Scala." The driver didn't linger but hurried away. She wondered how he'd get back, then decided it probably didn't matter. It was obvious that Bax had done this before.

"Gotta run. Stay safe," Bax repeated. He turned and headed up the stairs to the courthouse.

"I can't believe he paid for a guy to deliver a car." Liana gave Brock an exasperated look as she opened the passenger door. "Who does that?"

"It's a luxury," he admitted. "And unfortunately, this won't blend in the way Zeke's sedan had."

"Maybe that's for the better." She buckled her seat belt. "They probably won't expect us to show up in a brand-new vehicle."

"I just hope we don't wreck it," he muttered. "And I hope Bax paid for the insurance."

She hoped so too. His comment reminded her of the flash-bang. And how the assailant had tried to haul her away from the scene. "You really think we were found by using our disposable phones?"

Brock shrugged. "I honestly don't know how we were found there, but I would rather not take any chances."

She didn't want to risk being found again either. Her injured arm was a detriment as it was. She could still use her shooting hand, but she'd be handicapped if they had to climb more fences or squeeze in and out of basement windows.

She didn't want her physical limitations to put Brock in danger.

"You know, we lost sight of Dong and his buddy. We assumed they were walking back to the restaurant, but we never saw them again despite driving past. Maybe they had a car stashed nearby and followed us back to the hotel."

He frowned. "I guess that's possible."

"It's the only answer that makes sense," she insisted. The cold pack was losing its chill as the heated seats surrounded her with warmth. "They didn't know we'd broken into the basement."

"How would they recognize Zeke's car?" Brock asked.

"I think it's more likely Dong recognized me." She hesitated, then added, "Especially since he was in the kitchen the night you came in."

He grimaced. "It all comes back to the way I broke your cover. I'm so sorry, Liana."

"You already apologized." There was no point in rehashing the past. Sure, she had been upset at first. But if she were being honest, she'd tell him how glad she was to have his help and support.

And how much she'd missed him.

"Okay, the Lake View Motel is about three miles ahead." He'd programmed the address into the fancy GPS tracking system in the SUV's dashboard. "I'm going to drive past the place first so we can get a feel for we're dealing with."

In other words, how many girls might be held there, forced into doing unspeakable acts. She swallowed hard and silently prayed for God to grant her and Brock the wisdom and strength to rescue them.

When Brock slowly rolled past the motel, a flash of anger hit hard. The building and surrounding area looked worse than she'd imagined. This was so obviously a place that rented rooms by the hour, that it should have been eliminated a long time ago.

"I want to shut the motel down," she said, striving to remain calm. "I just know there are girls stationed in each of those horrible rooms."

"I feel the same way." He looked thoughtful as he went around the block. "I could call Rhy, see if we couldn't bring the entire team in to swarm the place."

"Based on what evidence?" She turned in her seat. "And what if we're wrong?"

"Do you think we're wrong?" Brock asked.

"No." She stared out the windshield. Brock pulled over to the side of the road a few yards from the motel. "An anonymous tip?"

The suggestion hung in the air between them.

"Okay, maybe we watch for a bit." She didn't like it, but she also didn't want to break the law by sending the tactical team in either. "If we see more than two men go into the same room, that's probable cause, right?"

"Right." He pulled his binocs out of his pocket. "You keep an eye on the parking lot. I'm heading out to get closer."

She didn't want him to leave her. Yet she swallowed her protest. "Fine. But if you're not back in fifteen minutes, I'm calling Rhy for backup."

"Deal." He flashed a smile as he slid out from behind the wheel. "Take my place," he added. "You may have to move the car."

"Okay." She slid out of the passenger seat, then went around to the driver's side. She took a moment to undo her sling, tossing it and the not-so-cold pack into the back seat.

Her arm still throbbed with pain, but the ibuprofen helped. She slid in behind the wheel, adjusted the seat, and picked up the binocs.

And steeled herself to watch.

For long moments, she didn't see anyone going in or out. Then a man left room number three. He seemed to glance around guiltily before walking away from the motel. There were very few cars in the parking lot, leading her to believe the so-called *customers* parked farther away.

Another five minutes passed before she saw another man emerge from room six. He didn't look guilty but smiled as he strolled away.

She wanted to smash her foot into his face.

A man at the corner of the building caught her eye. She moved the binocs to zoom in. Brock. Reminding herself he was armed, she turned her attention back to room three.

There. Another guy was walking across the parking lot, heading straight for room three. The minute he knocked at the door, and it cracked open, she felt her heart squeeze in her chest.

That was all she needed. She tried to get a glimpse of the woman who'd opened the door, but whoever it was stayed well out of sight.

This had to stop. She dug for her phone, intending to call Brock, only to realize he was already on his way.

And he was on the phone. She shoved out of the car to join him.

"Fifteen minutes? Got it. Thanks, Rhy." He lowered the phone. "We have backup coming in fifteen. Raelyn, Grayson, Zeke, Jina, and Flynn are on the way."

"Good. I want room three," she said.

He frowned. "You're injured. Let us take the lead."

She narrowed her gaze. "My op. I want room three."

He sighed, scrubbed his hand over his chin, then nodded. "Fine. It's yours."

Waiting fifteen minutes was excruciating. She consoled herself by knowing they'd be rescuing these girls very soon.

Thankfully, the team members began arriving a few minutes early. She'd met them before at their wedding and at other social functions too.

Their expressions grave, they gathered around her and Brock.

"We'll start in the lobby. I'll get master keys from the front desk." He nodded at her. "Liana wants room three. We'll spread out and enter the others simultaneously. Obviously, the goal is no shots fired, but all Johns will be arrested." He waited a beat. "Any questions?"

"Let's do it," Grayson said.

As a tight unit, they jogged toward the building. One man walking toward the motel abruptly stopped upon seeing them and bolted in the opposite direction.

Liana tensed. They didn't have much time.

Brock stormed into the lobby, holding up his badge and gun. "Freeze. Give us seven master key cards."

"I—uh," the clerk stammered.

"Do it," Brock barked. "Now."

Raelyn went around the counter to stand beside the clerk. The minute he coded seven key cards, Raelyn pushed them across the counter, then grabbed the clerk's hands, cuffing them behind him. "You're under arrest for aiding and abetting the criminal act of prostitution." She pushed him into a chair. "We'll be back."

Brock handed out the keys. Raelyn ran around to grab hers. "Ready?"

Liana was more than ready. She turned away and pushed through the lobby doors. She jogged to room three, pulled her weapon, and swiped the key card. "Police," she shouted as she opened the door.

A man was just putting his pants on when she burst in. "What in the . . ."

She threw him up against the wall, yanking his arms behind his back. She read him his rights as the woman got dressed.

One down and far too many more to go.

CHAPTER TEN

The takedown of the Lake View Motel was overall uneventful. No shots were fired, and they'd arrested several Johns. Brock noticed Liana going into each room to check on the girls. By the crestfallen expression on her face, none were Mai Shi.

Yet they were all free now. Some of the girls cried; others looked stoic as if they'd become accustomed to their roles and fully intended to return to it. He knew everyone couldn't be saved, but he hoped Liana, Raelyn, and Jina could convince them otherwise.

In an unusual approach, he and Rhy had agreed to treat the women as victims. Only the men were arrested. Until they understood how these girls had gotten mixed up in this, they would be taken to a shelter and provided food, clothing, and counseling.

"We've arrested twelve men," Grayson said. "Thirteen including the lobby clerk who keeps babbling about wanting a lawyer. So far, only one of these guys is willing to talk about how this operation was arranged. He claims they were to head to a storefront four blocks from here to pay, then were given a room number. No names were used, but we do have a description of a large Asian man who took his money and sent him here."

Brock glanced around in frustration. The biggest problem was that they didn't have anyone within the sex-trafficking ring in custody. "Grayson, I need you, Zeke, and Flynn to check out that storefront. I'm sure the large Asian is long gone but check anyway. Canvass the area. Maybe someone knows who he is. We need a name."

"Will do." Grayson gestured for Flynn and Zeke to join him. They took off moving quickly.

The female officers were still with the girls, and Brock didn't want to interrupt. Liana turned to glance at him, her eyes filled with pain.

He walked over, needing to offer whatever comfort he could. It wouldn't be enough. There was nothing he could do to erase what these women had suffered, but he prayed there was hope for their future.

Please, Lord, show them Your way.

"We need to find Twisted Snake," Liana said, moving away from the group. Raelyn and Jina were arranging for the girls to be transported to a nearby shelter. "I know he's behind this."

"Grayson, Zeke, and Flynn are checking the storefront." He understood and shared her desperate need to find this guy. "One of the Johns told us a large Asian man took his money and sent him here."

"The same man we saw last night?" She nodded thoughtfully. "If so, then the owners of the restaurant must be involved too. Otherwise, why would he have their car?"

"It's possible." He longed to pull her into his arms. "The

good news is that we now have probable cause to search the other properties owned by Lakeshore LLC."

Her expression brightened. "Can we be involved?"

He hesitated because Rhy had made it clear they could not tag along. Despite the work they'd done on the case, there was still the issue of Liana's cover being blown and the bad guys trying to kill her. "He wants us to go to a safe house."

"No. I'm not doing that." Her refusal was swift. "I don't report to Rhy. I intend to keep working this case."

He was afraid she'd say that. He inwardly sighed. "Okay, then that's what we'll do."

Her brow furrowed. "I don't want you to get in trouble with your boss," she protested.

He stared at her. "I'm not letting you do this alone, Liana. If you won't use the safe house, then I won't either."

She looked indecisive for a moment. "I'm sorry, Brock. I know I'm putting our lives in danger, but I can't ignore this." She waved a hand at the now-vacant motel. "I need to find those responsible and put them behind bars. If we don't, they'll just move and set up shop in a new location."

"I know, I want those responsible too." He reached for her right hand, frowning when he noticed her left wrist was still swollen. "We'll find them."

"How?" She glanced over at the various men who'd been arrested. "Can we get them to talk?"

"All but one has lawyered up." He grimaced. "And I don't think the Asian would give out his name, do you?"

She sighed. "So we're back to square one."

"The properties may reveal something," he said, although they already knew the two houses on Duckwood Drive held nothing of interest.

"Let's head back to the restaurant," Liana suggested. "I want to see if they're open for business."

He hesitated. "I need to wait until I hear from Grayson, Flynn, and Zeke. It's possible they'll have something for us to go on."

She reluctantly nodded. But his hopes dropped when two of the guys jogged back, their expressions grim.

"Several people admitted to seeing the large Chinese guy," Grayson said. "But no one knows his name or where he lives. He shows up every day on foot, so they haven't seen a vehicle either."

Brock wondered if the large Asian man used the owner's car during the daytime, parking it a few blocks from the storefront. He nodded at Grayson. "I need Gabe Melrose to check the cameras in that entire area for an SUV with the following license plate." He rattled the information off from memory. "He'll know what to look for."

"Got it," Grayson agreed, lifting his phone.

"Where's Zeke?" Brock asked.

"Waiting for the crime scene techs," Flynn explained. "We're hoping to find at least a few usable fingerprints to put through the system. If this guy has a criminal record, we have a better chance of finding him."

"Good work." He hoped the large Chinese man was in the system. "Can you wrap up things here? Liana and I need to head out."

Flynn and Grayson exchanged surprised glances. "Sure," Grayson said.

"Thanks." He took Liana's arm and steered her toward their rental car. "What makes you think Lu Chen's will be closed?"

"I'm worried they're packing up and moving their operation." She looked depressed as she slid into the passenger seat. "How had the Asian man known to take off once we'd hit the motel? Unless he had access to the cameras there and watched us invade the place."

It was a good point. He should have considered the ability of the Asian using the motel's camera. "Maybe we pulled the trigger too soon," he muttered. "Maybe if we'd scouted the place longer, we'd have him in custody."

"It wasn't too soon for those girls," she said with a tired sigh. "They deserve to be free."

"Yes, they do." He told himself not to focus on their failures, but on their success. He made it back to the restaurant in record time. And the minute he pulled up to the building, his heart sank.

The windows were dark. There were no cars in the small parking lot. And there was a white paper taped to the main doorway. Even from here he could see the word *Closed.*

"I knew it," Liana whispered. She shook her head in despair. "They bugged out like the creepy cockroaches they are."

On instinct, he kept going, heading for the two properties on Duckwood Drive. He didn't think the large Asian knew they'd been inside the home and might be using one or the other as a temporary hideout.

As he turned the corner, both residences appeared vacant. Scanning the street, he caught sight of the black SUV the Asian had been driving the night before.

"He's here?" Liana noticed it too. "Find a parking spot. Hurry."

Easier said than done; even in the middle of the day, cars lined the street. But he found a spot on the next block. He quickly parked, then called Grayson for backup. "Meet us on Duckwood Drive ASAP," he said. "I have reason to believe the large Asian is here. We're going inside using exigent circumstances."

"Roger that," Grayson agreed. "Wait for us."

Liana shook her head. "We're not waiting. We can't let him get away."

He nodded, unwilling to let the large Asian get away either. He doubted the guy was Twisted Snake, but eliminating another spoke in the wheel of this enterprise could help.

"I'll take the back," he said as they ran down the street. "You may not be able to get over the fence with your wrist. You cover the front."

She frowned but nodded. "Okay. Be careful, Brock."

"You too." He brought her in for a quick kiss before turning away. He cut through two backyards to reach the next street.

Time was of the essence. He wished now he hadn't told Grayson to repair the window. Thankfully, he still had the glass cutter.

Brock didn't worry about moving silently until he'd vaulted the fence, dropping down into the backyard of the house with the secret staircase. Like last night, he darted to the tree for cover, gazing at the windows, searching for signs of movement.

There was nothing. But that didn't mean someone wasn't inside. He hoped the Asian was in the house to the south so that he could use the secret staircase and catch him off guard.

He ran in a crouch to the basement window. Inspecting the caulk job, he decided to cut it away with the knife instead. Less than two minutes later, he was wiggling his way through the window. The step stool was right where they'd left it.

Listening intently, he didn't hear any movement from the main floor. He debated clearing the house, but then crossed to the panel door.

Opening it a crack, he heard voices again. Bingo. He crept up the stairs, thankful they were made of cement and therefore wouldn't creak or groan, alerting the men to his presence.

At least one, he thought as the voice became clearer. One man on the phone, maybe? Telling someone in charge about the bust on the motel? He had no way of knowing for sure.

And the person was speaking Chinese. He tried to concentrate on making sense of the words, but they were talking so fast he couldn't grasp what was being said. He wished Liana was here to translate.

Then again, better for her to be outside where it was safe. Grayson and Flynn would be there soon.

The voice suddenly stopped as if someone had hit a light switch. He froze, wondering if he'd been made, then continued moving, faster now.

What if they'd caught a glimpse of Liana?

He held his weapon ready as he continued through the passageway, fully expecting the Asian to bolt toward him at any moment. When the silence lengthened, he grew worried.

The sound of gunfire had him breaking into a run.

Liana!

WHEN THE LARGE Asian stepped through the front door, Liana knew there wasn't a moment to lose. Despite knowing their backup hadn't arrived yet, she sprang out from behind the SUV, and shouted, "Stop! Police!"

The large Asian had pulled a gun. She ducked behind the SUV as bullets slammed into the car. Peeking around the rear bumper, she took aim and returned fire.

The Asian darted to the right toward the house she and Brock had gone into the night before. He moved fast for being a big man.

No way was she going to lose him. Not this time. She ran behind the row of cars, keeping pace, ducking when he aimed his gun in her direction.

Brock shouted her name, but she ignored him. She fired at the Asian, hoping to slow him down.

They needed him alive!

He abruptly stopped and turned to fire back. She dropped to the ground as a bullet whizzed past her ear.

That was close. Her heart thudded in her chest, but she remained laser focused on the Asian. When he began to run, she jumped up and followed.

Brock came running toward him too. Seeing him gave her the jolt of confidence she needed to put on a burst of speed. Adrenaline raced through her blood stream as she threw herself on top of the big Asian.

They hit the ground hard, the breath leaving her lungs in a painful whoosh. Momentum carried them forward, rolling over and over until the big man was on top, crushing her.

He shouted obscenities, surprisingly in English. He wrapped his giant hands around her throat, cutting off what little air she had left.

Looking up into his red and angry face, she realized she was going to die.

Then Brock was there, yanking the man off her and

slapping handcuffs onto his wrists. She gasped for air, unable to move. Sprawled on someone's front lawn, she stared up at the sky, dazed.

Her entire body felt as if she'd been beaten with a sledgehammer.

Or a giant Asian.

She wanted to laugh or cry. But it took all her concentration just to breathe. She heard more voices indicating Brock's backup had arrived.

"Liana?" Brock's concerned face hovered above her. "Don't move. There's an ambulance on the way."

"I—don't need an ambulance." She managed to push the words past her sore throat. "Help me up."

"You shouldn't move," he said. "You may have broken bones."

"I don't." At least, she didn't think so. "Please, Brock. I need to sit up."

With obvious reluctance, he slipped his arm beneath her shoulders and helped her into a sitting position. "Thanks," she croaked. "It's easier to breathe now."

"You shouldn't have done that." His features still reflected concern. "That guy is built like a tank."

"Trust me. I'm aware." She put her good hand to her throat, then frowned. "Where's my gun?"

"Here." Grayson came over to kneel beside her. "You took that guy down like a pro football linebacker."

"Thanks." She assumed it was a compliment, although she didn't know much about football. She looked past Grayson and Brock to the Asian. "Do we have his name?"

"Not yet." Brock shrugged. "We're booking him on attempted murder and on sex trafficking. The charges for the latter may not stick without corroboration from the Johns, but all that matters is that he won't get bail."

"He should be placed in protective custody." She swallowed against the pain in her throat. "Remember Bai Chow?"

"Yeah, trust me, we'll make sure of that," Brock assured her.

The Asian glanced at her when she mentioned Bai. She held his gaze. "If you're smart, you'll tell us where to find Twisted Snake," she said in Mandarin. "He's the one we want. You're just a pawn."

The big man looked away without saying anything in return. She hoped he'd consider giving them the information they needed.

But she also didn't want to wait too long either. The vacant expression on some of those girls' faces haunted her. They'd been through so much.

And there were others they had yet to find.

Mai Shi.

The wail of an ambulance siren made her groan. She looked at Brock. "Help me up, please?"

He did so, taking her hand and lifting her upright without her help. Her muscles tightened in protest, and she patted her pocket with her good hand, looking for the ibuprofen.

"Here." Reading her mind, Brock opened a bottle and tapped four tablets into her hand. It was probably too soon, but she tossed them back anyway.

"I'm fine. I don't need to go to the hospital." She glanced at the Asian, but he looked away.

She was glad they had him, but they needed more. She turned to look down the street at the two homes owned by Lakeshore LLC.

"We need to get to those other properties ASAP," she said to Brock, "before they're abandoned as well."

"Yes, Rhy has sent officers to all locations," he confirmed. "Hopefully, we'll find a few more players who will be more willing to talk." He looked directly at the Asian. "First to talk gets the deal."

The big man remained stubbornly silent.

She tried not to feel deflated. They'd done great work today. First busting up the motel sex operation and then arresting one of the major players.

At least, she hoped the Asian was a major player.

"What about the restaurant owners, Yuze and Lin Lu Chen?" She turned to Brock. "They own the SUV that the Asian was driving. He tried to kill me. Does that give us probable cause to arrest them? Or at least issue a BOLO as persons of interest?"

"Yeah, it does." He nodded at Grayson who stepped away to call Rhy, updating him on their progress. "Do you think Yuze is Twisted Snake?"

She sighed, glancing again at the Asian in cuffs. He stared off into the distance as if he didn't understand a word of English, although she knew very well that he did. He'd cursed at her in English after all. "I doubt it, but anything is possible."

The ambulance rolled toward her, along with a police cruiser. She wouldn't have minded some ice for her throat and maybe for her left wrist, which was throbbing painfully again, but she wasn't going to the hospital.

Her injuries were nothing compared to what those poor girls had suffered.

The scene grew chaotic as more uniformed officers swarmed the area. It was, after all, their jurisdiction. She winced, knowing Rhy's team would get some heat for infringing on another precinct's turf.

Not that she cared. Getting the Asian in custody was worth it.

Glancing at Brock, she could tell he felt the same way. He brought the EMTs toward her. "Liana needs to be evaluated. The guy in custody tried to choke her. And she has a badly injured wrist."

The EMTs examined her throat, checked her oxygenation levels in her blood, and then looked at her wrist. "This needs X-rays," the older of the two told her.

"I know. I'll get it checked out soon." But not now. "Do you have an ice pack you can spare?"

"Take two," the EMT said, handing them over.

"Thanks." She placed one over her wrist and held the other to her throat. She and Brock couldn't leave until the officers had taken their statements, but she was anxious to know if anyone was taken into custody at the other properties.

Almost two hours passed before she, Brock, Grayson, Zeke, and Flynn were free to leave. Brock hadn't been happy about her refusal to go to the hospital, but she'd signed the waiver anyway, knowing full well he'd have done the same thing if the situation was reversed.

Men. Sometimes they could be so—*annoying*.

"We need a safe place to hang out for a short while," Brock said to Grayson.

"Why not use the safe house Rhy arranged?" Grayson darted a glance at her. "I mean, you don't have to stay there, but it's probably better than a hotel."

"I'd rather stay someplace nearby." She felt certain that if she agreed to the safe house, Brock would make sure they never left. "We may need to head out to one of the other properties."

Grayson shrugged and looked at Brock as if saying, "She's your problem, dude." And wasn't that the truth?

"I wouldn't mind getting something to eat," Brock said. "It's been hours since breakfast."

She didn't have much of an appetite, but a restaurant was better than a safe house. "That's fine with me."

"Do you want us to come with you?" Flynn asked. "Looks like you could use some additional protection."

"No need," Brock assured them. "I'd rather you guys continue feeding us information on the investigation. We still don't know who the Asian is or where to find Twisted Snake."

"Understood," Zeke agreed. "We can do that."

"Yep." Flynn nodded. "But I still think you could use a bodyguard or two," he added, eyeing the Asian who was being stuffed into the back of a squad. "I hope there aren't more like him out there."

"You and me both," Liana said. The ice pack had helped reduce the swelling in her neck and her arm, but it was still painful to talk. And swallow.

A cold chocolate malt suddenly sounded good.

Brock looped his arm around her shoulders, keeping her close as they made their way to the SUV Bax had arranged for them. She longed for a long, hot bath, but she knew if she said anything, she'd end up at the safe house.

The police presence diminished enough that they were able to drive away. She rested against the seat, reveling in the warmth seeping up through the seat cushions. Next best thing for aching muscles.

"Can we go to Kones?" It was the best frozen custard and butter hamburger joint restaurant in the area. And had been one of their favorite spots.

"Sure." He shot her a surprised look. "We used to go there for special occasions."

"We're alive, aren't we?" She managed a weak smile. "That's a special occasion. And I'd really love one of their thick malt shakes."

"Sounds good to me."

They drove in silence for several minutes. She was exhausted, not just physically from bouncing off the large Asian but emotionally.

It was impossible to get those poor girls out of her mind.

When Brock pulled into the driveway of Kones, she tried to focus on the positive. For the first time in months, they were making progress. Not as much as she'd like, but some movement against the sex-trafficking ring was better than none.

Brock snagged a small table for two, gesturing for her to sit. "I'll order for us. You want a burger too?"

"Sure." She wasn't sure how much of it she'd be able to eat, but they were delicious. He placed their order, bringing two shakes and a number plaque to the table.

"Do you mind if I say grace this time?" She didn't know much about praying, but she felt the need to do this.

"Of course." He took her uninjured hand in his, kissed it, then bowed his head.

"Lord Jesus, we thank You for this food. And we ask that You please heal the wounds of those girls who suffered today. Bring them peace, hope, and safety. Amen."

"Amen," Brock murmured.

She sipped her malt, the cold ice-cream drink feeling wonderful on her throat. She glanced up expectantly when Brock's phone rang.

"What's up, Rhy?"

The color drained from Brock's face as he listened.

"You're serious?" His voice sounded strained. His green gaze locked on hers. "Yes, I'll tell her. Thanks."

"What?" She braced herself for the bad news.

"The Asian is dead. The squad was hit by gunfire before they reached the precinct."

Dead. Just like Bai Chow. Murdered to keep him from talking.

Despair hit hard. At this rate, they'd never find the man known only as Twisted Snake.

CHAPTER ELEVEN

Brock couldn't believe the Asian was dead. Killed before he could even be booked on charges. How in the world had that happened?

A sudden chill ran down his spine. "Lieutenant Troy Wallace."

"What about him?" Liana asked. Then she frowned. "You still think he's involved? That he somehow orchestrated this recent murder?"

"Yeah, I do." He'd never liked the guy; granted, he'd never met the guy either. He accepted the fact that Liana hadn't been sleeping with him. Brock knew it was well past time to let his old anger and resentment go.

But not if Wallace happened to be a dirty cop.

Their meals arrived, and he dug into his cheeseburger ravenously. Liana took a small bite of hers, and he wondered for like the tenth time if he should forcibly take her to the hospital for treatment.

"I don't know about that," Liana said with a frown between bites. "Why would Troy ask me to go undercover to bust up the organization if he's a part of it? That doesn't make any sense."

She had a point, but the Asian's murder was no coincidence. "I'm not sure. Maybe the goal was to include you in the sex-trafficking ring too. As one of the girls."

"Four months, Brock," she reminded him. "And that never happened." She grimaced, then added, "Well, not until the flash-bang attempt to grab me outside City Central. But they easily could have done that much sooner if that was the end goal."

"Okay, someone else, then." He still believed Troy was involved, but arguing wouldn't help. It irked him she was so defensive of the guy. "Someone Troy works for. Maybe his boss knows about your role."

"We discussed that before, remember? Captain Jorge Marbury." She slowly shook her head. "All anyone knows is that I was officially placed on an extended medical leave. Only Marbury and Wallace know the truth about my undercover assignment."

She was right, Marbury was more likely the leak. Yet her point was valid. Why assign anyone to the case if things within the sex-trafficking organization were humming along? They were missing a key point to this. But what?

"We need to talk to Rhy." As he said the words, it struck him how often he leaned on his fellow teammates, enjoying a camaraderie Liana hadn't experienced in months of working undercover.

Guilt hit hard. All this time he'd thought the worst, imagining her with Troy or even some other guy. When she'd been tirelessly working to break up what may be the largest sex-trafficking ring in the city.

While attending church with Joe and Steele, he'd learned about forgiveness. But forgiving himself for his lack of faith in Liana wasn't easy. He never should have accused her of cheating on him.

She arched a brow. "What can Rhy do? Other than involve someone from internal affairs to see if Marbury has any dirt on him."

It was another good point. "I guess I'm hoping Rhy can do a little research on his own first. I don't see how we can get IAB looped in without proof."

She took another small bite of her burger, then reached for her shake. There was the slightest grimace on her features when she swallowed. "I'd like to head over to the other Lakeshore LLC properties when we're finished here."

"Are you sure you're okay?" He'd lost it when he saw the large Asian's hands locked around her neck. Only knowing the guy was more valuable alive than dead kept him from shooting him on the spot.

In hindsight, he wished he had. The Asian had given them nothing and was dead anyway. And Liana's throat was still bruised and sore. "What if the swelling gets worse?"

"I'll let you know if that's a concern." She sighed and reached across the table with her good arm. "I promise I'm fine."

She'd been through the ringer this morning, first the flash-bang, then being nearly choked to death, but he forced himself to let it go. This was her case, and it was personal.

For him, too, now.

They finished their meal. Liana only ate half her burger, and the way she eyed the empty shake, he could tell she wanted another. "One for the road?"

"That would be great." She lifted a hand to her neck. "They're soothing on my throat."

He nodded. He placed her order, then handed her the large shake. They headed out to the SUV.

Going to the other properties would likely prove fruitless. Yet he knew she'd balk at going to the safe house, even temporarily. Leaning over, he punched in the address to a home roughly two miles from the properties on Duckwood Drive.

Once they were on the road, he called Rhy, placing the call on speaker. "We need some intel."

"Let me guess, you want to know if Captain Jorge Marbury or Lieutenant Troy Wallace might be working for the bad guys."

He had to grin. It was nice to know they were on the same page. "Yep. Only someone working on the inside could have arranged for a shooter to take the Asian out of commission that fast."

"I considered that too. On the surface, these guys are solid. No hint of scandal with either of them."

Of course, it couldn't be easy. He sighed. "Then who?"

"Don't know. I'm trying to dig deeper. But we were finally able to get the Asian's prints in the system," Rhy said. "His name is Xiong Mihn. Liana? Does that ring a bell?"

Liana shook her head. "Afraid not."

"He was arrested several years ago for assault, but didn't do much time," Rhy continued. "He was here on a work visa and supposed to be deported back to China. Apparently, that didn't happen."

"Maybe he did time with someone who was part of the sex-trafficking organization?" he suggested.

"That's possible. I'll ask Gabe to pull some names." There was a brief pause before Rhy added, "Did you get to the safe house yet?"

"Not exactly." He glanced pointedly at Liana who shrugged. "We thought we'd swing by the other Lakeshore LLC properties first."

"Don't bother," Rhy said. "I just heard from the team that all properties are vacant. They're searching them now, but so far, they haven't found anything left behind."

"Not even fingerprints?" Liana asked.

"We've sent crime scene techs out to dust for prints. Who knows? Maybe we'll get a lead there."

Only if they were already in the system. Like Xiong. He swallowed his frustration. Their only lead had been silenced.

"What about Yuze and Lin Lu Chen?" she asked. "We know they loaned a vehicle to Xiong. They're likely a part of this. And there's Muchin too. Although without a second name, it will be more difficult to find him."

"We're looking for all three, but especially Yuze and Lin," Rhy said. "We'd hoped to find them at one of the other properties listed as being owned by Lakeshore LLC, but so far, they're still in the wind. A search on Muchin's name in the database didn't reveal anyone being arrested by that name."

Too many dead ends, he thought grimly. They had to be missing something. But what? They'd followed every lead they had.

Without anything to show for it. No, that wasn't true. They had rescued those girls from the motel.

"Rhy, will you keep us informed?" Liana asked.

"Of course. Head to the safe house." Rhy issued the directive like an order.

"We'll be in touch." He gestured for Liana to end the call. "That wasn't a suggestion, you know. He's dead serious."

"So am I," she said. "I think we should head back to Lu Chen's. I know it's closed, but maybe we can find something Bai left behind."

He inwardly sighed but made the turn to head in that direction. He'd considered going in earlier, but then they had gone to the properties on Duckwood. Which had been the right call, as they'd found Xiong. It couldn't hurt to check the restaurant. Fingerprints would be useless, there would be far too many to wade through. But would they find something else? Maybe. "Okay, but if we don't uncover any leads, we head to the safe house."

She wrinkled her nose, then reluctantly nodded. "I don't know what else to do. We can't talk to the female victims from the motel yet, they need time to recover. And I doubt they'll know anything about Twisted Snake anyway. He's at the top of the organization. Their interaction was likely with Bai Chow or Xiong Mihn."

And neither of those men would be telling them anything.

"I've been praying for those girls," Liana said. "It's really hard for me to understand why God had allowed such horrible things to happen."

"I know. Every time I mentioned that to Joe, Steele, or Rhy, they reminded me that it's not up to us to question God's plan. To question why some people suffer so much more than others." It was times like this that maintaining faith was difficult. "This life on earth isn't the most important thing, it's how we give ourselves to the Lord for everlasting life."

Liana was silent for a long moment. "I guess I have a lot to learn."

"Me too." He reached for her hand. Her left wrist was still swollen and wrapped, so he only covered her fingers gently. "Maybe when this is over, we can learn together."

She glanced at him in surprise. This was the first time either of them mentioned what their relationship might look like when they had found and arrested Twisted Snake.

Would Liana want to push forward with the divorce?

Or was there a possibility they could try again?

He was shocked at how badly he wanted the chance to try again. To be a better husband this time.

"Maybe," she agreed softly, making his heart soar with hope.

All they needed to do was to stay alive.

LIANA COULD HARDLY BELIEVE Brock had suggested they attend church together when this case was over.

Just church? Or more?

Picking up where they'd left off wouldn't be easy. She had been surprised to learn they were still married, but only because he hadn't gotten around to filing against her. Hadn't he admitted to making several appointments to file for their divorce? The fact remained that Brock hadn't trusted her. And she'd basically proven him right by leaving without saying a word or following up with him afterward.

But simply working this case didn't mean he'd miraculously trust her again.

She told herself this wasn't the time to think about their future. They had much bigger problems ahead of them.

Was he right about Lieutenant Troy Wallace or his boss, Captain Jorge Marbury? She didn't want to believe either of them could be involved in the sex-trafficking organization. Yet there was no denying Xiong's murder happening so soon after his arrest was suspicious.

Was this an inside job? Or not? Getting access to a

police scanner wasn't difficult. It was just as likely that Twisted Snake and his people had heard about the Asian's arrest and had moved quickly to eliminate him as a threat.

Leaving them with nothing to go on. Even this trip to Lu Chen's wasn't likely to yield anything helpful. Not when others had already been there.

But she couldn't stand sitting around and doing nothing. Not after busting up the ring at the Lake View Motel.

If the kitchen help were more involved in running the organization than she'd realized, it was possible they'd left something behind.

What? She had no clue.

Taking another long sip of her chocolate malt, she relished the coolness on her throat. She didn't need to look in a mirror, she knew bruises were already starting to form. And the inside of her throat was raw too. The EMTs hadn't been happy she'd refused transport to the hospital, yet they had instructed her to get to the emergency department right away if the swelling reached a point where it impacted her breathing.

She took a moment to draw in a deep breath, then let it out.

So far, so good.

They'd also rewrapped her wrist and given her two more ice packs. Her wrist felt much better. Or maybe it was just getting easier to ignore the pain. She couldn't afford to allow her injuries to sideline her.

The more she thought about a cop being involved, the less she believed it. For all they knew, Twisted Snake had someone watching the motel from afar. Or keeping an eye on the properties on Duckwood. It could even have been the tattooed guy who'd shot at them from her apartment window. At the time, she'd thought Tattoo Guy had been hired by Xiong.

Now she felt certain he'd been hired by Twisted Snake himself. She considered asking Brock to return to her apartment, then decided against it. She highly doubted Tattoo Guy was waiting there.

It was also possible Yuze and Lin Lu Chen had hired Tattoo Guy. Maybe she was wrong about Yuze not being Twisted Snake. The rumors of the snake tattoos on his arms could be grossly exaggerated. Rhy had issued BOLOs for them, though, so there wasn't anything else they could do but wait for them to be picked up.

The keen sense of frustration wouldn't leave her alone. They needed something to go on. Anything.

Please, Lord, guide us to the truth!

As before, the prayer came unbidden, echoing in her mind before she even realized it. Disconcerted, she glanced at Brock, who appeared lost in his own thoughts.

When he pulled into Lu Chen's parking lot, the restaurant looked as forlorn as earlier. Hard to believe she and Brock had spent happy evenings here, completely clueless as to the rotten underbelly of sex trafficking going on there.

She wished more than anything she could have found something useful during her time working undercover. She felt like a failure. And those poor girls had paid the ultimate price.

Then she straightened in her seat, doing her best to push the negativity from her mind. No point in rehashing the past. There was no way she could have known about the illegal meetings taking place in the kitchen. Or in Bai's office.

All the more reason she wanted to get back inside the place now.

"Looks like the cops already searched the place," Brock said, nodding at the police tape stretched across the door.

"I still want to go inside." She knew she was being obstinate, but she refused to back down. Her meetings with Bai Chow were brief, except for the last one, when Brock had burst into the kitchen. But she knew Bai must have met with plenty of others. And where was Dong and the other kitchen staff? Had they all been let go?

Or had they been moved to some other aspect of the operation?

She slid out of the passenger seat and followed Brock to the door. He removed the tape and jiggled the door handle. It was locked.

Undeterred, he pulled the handful of tools from his pocket. Within five minutes, he'd jimmied the door handle to the point they could get inside.

"Handy," she said, stepping across the threshold. The scent of ginger, soy sauce, peanuts, and garlic still hung in the air.

Brock closed the door behind them. The interior was cool, the heat likely turned off when the employees had left.

"You want to start in the kitchen?" Brock asked.

"Let's check Bai's office first." She led the way to a room that was no bigger than a closet. The desk was small, and the computer that normally sat on top of the pocked surface was gone.

She quickly checked the drawers; all were empty. She even checked the Chinese painting on the wall. There wasn't anything behind it. Then she dropped to her hands and knees, inspecting the floor.

Still nothing.

With a sigh, she stood and glanced around, trying to imagine where else Bai could have hidden something important. But there was nothing that resembled a secret drawer or cubbyhole.

"Okay," she said, turning away and flashing Brock a rueful smile. "Time to check the kitchen."

Thankfully, he followed her to the much larger space without saying *I told you so*.

To her surprise, many of the pots and pans and utensils were still there. "Do you want to start on that side?" She gestured to the left. "I'll take this side."

"Works for me." Brock turned away to start in the corner.

She did the same on the opposite end. They worked in silence for long minutes. She searched every shelf, every drawer, every pot and pan.

Searching the kitchen took much longer, as there were far too many nooks and crannies. She wondered if the cops who'd searched the place earlier had been this thorough, then decided it didn't matter.

She would have come here again no matter what they had or hadn't found.

"I've got nothing," Brock said, breaking the silence. "You?"

"Nothing." She turned toward the supply closet. "Give me a minute to check this too."

"I can help." He came over to stand beside her.

"It's tight in here." She glanced over her shoulder. "But I appreciate the support."

"I'll go through the bathrooms." He shrugged. "May as well be thorough."

A man after her own heart. Turning back to the matter at hand, she moved the food supplies from the shelves, checking the wall behind them.

Again finding nothing.

Was she wrong about the restaurant? She sighed and stood, rubbing her swollen wrist. All the lifting and shoving was aggravating her injury.

As she headed into the cleaning area of the kitchen, Brock joined her. She glanced through the dish machine, then poked a long-handled spoon at the stinky garbage that had been left behind. Deciding against going through it, she headed for the two large doors located at the far end of the room. The first one was a walk-in freezer.

"Will you prop the door open?" She glanced at Brock. "I don't want to get locked in here."

"No problem." He pulled the stinky garbage can over and set it up against the door.

She stepped inside and scanned the large boxes of frozen goods. She moved several of them, making sure there was nothing hidden behind them. She frowned at the amount of food that had been left behind. She didn't like knowing it may all go to waste.

Probably not something that mattered to the owners, though. Sex trafficking likely paid better than running a Chinese restaurant.

She forced herself to go through the entire freezer before joining Brock. Shivering, she pushed the garbage can away with her foot and allowed the door to close. "One more," she said, gesturing to the next door.

He nodded and pulled the door open. This was a refrigerated cooler. She stepped inside, waiting for a moment for Brock to prop that door open too. There was less food in here, so it didn't take nearly as long to get through the shelves.

Along the farthest wall, there were plastic sheets hanging from the ceiling to the floor. She walked over and brushed them aside.

And found another door.

"Brock?" she whispered, her pulse kicking into high gear. "Do you see this?"

"Yeah." He kept his voice low too. "We need backup."

"We don't know that there's anything behind it," she protested. Yet the door reminded her of the secret passage they'd found behind the fake paneling, a staircase joining one house to the next. "Let's just take a peek."

"Me first." He gently elbowed her out of the way.

She bit back a sigh and stepped to the side. He pulled his weapon, then reached for the door.

Holding her weapon ready, too, she held her breath as the door opened with a soft snick. After a long moment of silence, she craned her neck to see around him.

Stairs leading down into what appeared to be a long tunnel. If there were lights along the way, they weren't on now.

"Stay behind me," he said in a low voice.

Since he had two good hands compared to her one, she reluctantly nodded. Besides, her left arm was throbbing worse thanks to her exhaustive search of the restaurant kitchen.

She stayed close as he silently made his way into the tunnel. Then she tugged on the back of his jacket, stopping him. When he glanced back at her, she gestured toward the door. Nodding in understanding, he waited for her to prop the door open behind them before they continued following the path ahead.

She nearly gasped when he clicked one of the small flashlights, illuminating the space ahead.

The tunnel was longer than she'd expected. She tried to imagine the area outside, anticipating where this tunnel would lead. Underground for sure, considering they'd taken stairs down from the kitchen level.

This time, there were no muted voices indicating the tunnel was occupied. Yet she understood there could still be bad guys waiting for them on the other end of the passageway.

From the height and width of the passageway, it had clearly been there for years, not something made recently. It was all too easy to imagine Bai Chow, Xiong, or others using the tunnel to get from one location to the next. It was a little surprising they hadn't taken her through here at one point or another.

Maybe she hadn't been as deeply entrenched in the organization as she'd thought.

After they'd gone roughly fifty yards, give or take, Brock abruptly slowed. Peering over his shoulder, she caught a glimpse of another couple of steps leading to a door.

He turned, placing his mouth near her ear. "Head back and call Rhy for backup."

"If you're going in, I'm going."

He hesitated, obviously torn. Then he took the last few steps to reach the door. He pressed against it, opening it a half an inch.

Nothing happened.

Brock pushed the door open farther, looking through the opening. Then he quickly backed out, letting the door close softly.

"Hurry," he whispered hoarsely. She instinctively turned to retrace their steps, braced for the sound of gunfire.

CHAPTER TWELVE

When Brock had glimpsed girls huddled together inside the room along with the tattooed guy holding a gun aimed in their direction, he knew he had to get Liana out of there. The tattooed guy hadn't seemed to notice the door opening a crack, his gaze was fixated on the girls, but he didn't want to take any chances.

It was good for them that Tattoo Guy wasn't very observant. Brock needed the rest of the tactical team to help get all the innocent victims out safely. Rhy would likely give him grief over exploring the passageway without having the team there.

But he'd agreed with Liana that it was better to know what they were up against. Honestly, his biggest concern was getting Liana out of the tunnel without her putting up a fight and insisting on staying.

When they reached Lu Chen's walk-in cooler, he softly closed that door behind them. No sense in alerting anyone they'd been inside. He gestured for Liana to follow as he headed through the kitchen and out through the back door.

"What did you see?" Liana grabbed his arm, her dark eyes intense. "Why did we leave?"

"The tattoo guy is inside, armed and apparently guarding several girls. We found them, Liana, or at least some of them. But we need backup." He lifted his phone and called Rhy. His boss answered on the second ring.

"What's going on, Brock?"

"I found more girls being held in a room probably three to four blocks from Lu Chen's restaurant. We need the team here ASAP."

"I'll send out the alert, but where exactly are they being held?" Rhy asked. "Can we safely get them out of the location?"

Two very good questions. He quickly explained about the passageway through the back of the walk-in cooler, leading to another building.

"You're saying the police missed it?" Rhy asked incredulously.

"Easy to miss, it's not obvious. And they weren't looking for a secret passage." Brock knew that if they hadn't found the one in the house on Duckwood, he may not have looked behind the wall of plastic either. "That doesn't matter now. We found the passageway, and I saw at least five girls, maybe more, in a room with at least one armed guard. Same guy who took shots at us from Liana's apartment." He tried to think back. Was that yesterday? He felt as if they were in a time warp with so much going on. An idea hit. "We know the one house on Duckwood Drive is owned by a David Kimball. That could be our Tattoo Guy. Or maybe he's a friend of Tattoo Guy."

"Okay, that's good work," Rhy said. "I'll put the team on notice."

"Thanks. Liana and I will scout the area while we're waiting for the others to arrive. We know the tunnel went to the south. There are only a couple of buildings in that direction. We'll narrow down which one is being used by these guys."

"I'll be there soon," Rhy said. "It's fine you check the properties, but don't engage, do you hear me? Wait until we all get there, understand?"

"I hear you. But stay in touch. We can't have dozens of armed cops converging on the area." A quick glance around confirmed there wasn't any place close by to hide the team. "We need a location several blocks away to use as a staging area. Most likely to the east of the building involved. And maybe one or two people covering Lu Chen's."

"Agree. Scout for a place for that, too, once you've identified the building. Our team is all over the city, so it's going to take time to get everyone together."

Liana frowned, clearly listening in. He understood her impatience to get the girls out of there, but they couldn't ignore the armed guard. Where there was one, there was likely more. Using the team had worked well at the Lake View Motel.

It would work here too.

"We will. Thanks." He lowered the phone, shoving it back into his pocket. "This way," he said, heading south.

To her credit, she didn't protest. He wrapped his arm around her shoulder, holding her close. The sky was clear, the air crisp coming off the lake. Not exactly a great day for a romantic stroll, but he was still hoping they wouldn't attract attention.

The first building next to the restaurant was another restaurant. He noticed it was closer to the road, with a larger parking lot in the back. By his estimation, the tunnel from Lu Chen's kitchen had to be located beneath the parking lot. That was the right angle, and besides, these two restaurants were too close together. He and Liana had gone at least fifty yards before reaching the other end of the tunnel.

As they continued walking, he eyed the next closest building to the restaurant. It was a two-story structure that looked as if it had once been a café on the lower level with living space up above but was clearly not being used now. It appeared abandoned—some of the windows were boarded up, and no lights were visible through the windows that weren't covered with wood or newspaper.

And no sign of activity within.

He could easily imagine the sex traffickers using the place as a hideout, a temporary staging location before moving the girls elsewhere. At least they'd taken the Lake View Motel out of the picture, but he wasn't under any illusion that there weren't others.

Too many other possibilities where they could exploit these girls.

Yet there was no way to know for sure this was the location, so he urged Liana forward toward the third building. This one had a sign indicating it was once a shoe store. Unfortunately, this place also appeared abandoned. Similar to the other one, although much more dilapidated. Even from here, he could see the sign indicating it was declared unsafe and scheduled for demolition.

He frowned. Which one was being used by the sex traffickers? Both? Maybe.

They strolled past, turned the corner at the next intersection, and headed east, toward the lakefront. When they were out of the sight line from either building, he huddled along the side of a trendy coffee shop and turned to face Liana.

"I'm not sure which of the two buildings is our target," he confessed. "My gut says the structure closer to the restaurant is more likely, but if we're wrong . . ." He didn't finish.

They couldn't afford to be wrong. Not in this.

"I agree with your gut. We need to find a way to peek inside the former shoe store first," she said. "I'll do it."

"No, you stay here." He wanted to groan at the flash of annoyance in her eyes. "Look, you're a great cop, Liana. But you're injured and probably far more recognizable to the tattoo guy than I am." *And more recognizable to Muchin*, he thought, hoping Liana's former criminal boss was inside. "See if you can find a reasonable position along here to use as a staging area. The coffee shop doesn't offer a line of sight to the buildings. But there may be something farther down that would work. Here, take Rhy's cell number and let him know what you find." He rattled off the information, which she dutifully entered into her phone. When she finished, he pulled her in for a hug. "I won't be long."

To his surprise, she clung to him as if she needed the physical connection too. But it was over far too quickly. She stepped back and eyed him sternly. "Go. But if you're not back in fifteen, I'm coming after you."

"Okay." Arguing would be useless. And he fully intended to be quick. He left her at the coffee shop and retraced their steps.

The area along the front of the shoe store was deserted, not a surprise since the only place open for business was the restaurant near Lu Chen's. And that wasn't very crowded. He slipped around back and pressed himself against the brick building.

Two of the windows were boarded up, but the third one wasn't. The glass was thick with dirt, though, and he couldn't see much even cupping his hands around his face to block out the light.

Moving to the back door, he tried the handle. Locked. He put his ear against the warped wood and listened. Hearing nothing, he pulled out his tools and went to work, hoping and praying he wasn't alerting the bad guys hiding inside.

If he'd guessed wrong, bullets could blast through the door at any second.

Thankfully, there was nothing but silence as he worked. He tried to keep an eye on his watch, knowing Liana would make good on her threat. After five minutes, he managed to get the door open. He winced when it creaked loudly.

He paused, staying back, then tentatively moved forward, carefully pushing the door inward. Rank air greeted him, making him wrinkle his nose. He doubted the sex traffickers were inside with that stench but stepped across the threshold anyway.

The interior was dark. It took a moment for his eyes to adjust. A thick layer of dust coated the few shelves and cabinets inside, and mice scurried across the floor at his feet.

No one had been in there for a long time. At least, not on this level. But the basement?

Moving through an open area that had once been a storefront, he searched for other doorways. There had to be one leading up to the second level, the other down to the basement. He found them around the corner, two doors side by side.

He listened again. Still nothing. He opened the first door; there were steps leading down to a dark basement. Flipping on his penlight, he scanned the area below. No footprints in the dust on the floor. At least, not human ones. Rodents aplenty, though, he noted.

Taking the steps halfway down, he swept the beam of the light from side to side. The entire area was empty.

Clearly, the sex traffickers were not using this in any capacity. The girls must be in the building to the north of this one, the former café with living space above. He was glad they'd taken the time to rule one location out.

Brock quickly turned and headed up the stairs to the main level. Another glance at his watch confirmed he had a full five minutes left before Liana would try to find him.

But he froze when the back door he'd left ajar suddenly closed. The wind? He pressed his back against the wall and waited.

A long minute passed before he breathed easier. Had to be the wind. He quickly darted to the door and peered through the opening between the warped door and the frame. Seeing nothing alarming, he opened the door farther and slid out.

Time to head back to Liana.

He was anxious for the rest of the tactical team to arrive. Not just to rescue the girls, which was important, but also to get their hands on Tattoo Guy.

And hopefully either Muchin or Twisted Snake.

He wanted to blow a hole in this organization so wide it could never be resurrected again by anyone else.

Ever.

WAITING for Brock was pure torture. Liana did her best to stay busy, finding the perfect location, in her estimation, for the tactical team to set up.

Three blocks to the north of the coffee shop, she found a tall two-story restaurant building. The Foxhound was open for lunch and dinner. It looked nice enough, but when she spoke to the manager, she learned they had a booming business hosting small weddings. The entire roof of the restaurant had been converted into a partially covered patio.

"Really?" Liana gushed. "My fiancée and I are looking for a place to hold a small wedding. Can I see the rooftop space?"

"Of course, follow me." The manager led the way up a set of stairs, pointing out they even had elevator access too.

When Liana stepped outside, she couldn't help but smile. Walking to the southwest, she discovered there was a direct line of sight to both allegedly deserted buildings.

The perfect location for a sniper.

After thanking the woman and promising to be in touch, Liana left the restaurant and hurried back to the coffee shop. She called Rhy, instructing him on the name of the Foxhound restaurant and the rooftop access.

"Thanks, Liana, that sounds good. Where's Brock?"

"Still scouting the two abandoned buildings." She checked her watch, frowning when she realized Brock's time was nearly up. "I'm sure he'll be back soon."

"We'll meet you at the Foxhound restaurant, okay?"

"Yes, that works. See you soon." She disconnected from the call, then glanced around.

Had something happened? Brock was armed and fully capable of taking care of himself, but she decided to head in that direction, planning to meet up with him halfway.

She crossed the street, then darted down two blocks to get closer. At that corner, she glanced down the road that led past the front doors of both structures.

Hmm. Still no sign of Brock. Had she missed him?

Movement caught her eye. Her gaze narrowed on the skinny man who was walking quickly along the other side of the road. His head was ducked against the wind, but his profile was distinctly Asian. He looked familiar, then she recognized the chief cook, Dong.

She hesitated, then followed, keeping far enough back that he hopefully wouldn't see her. Her pulse spiked with anticipation as he crossed the street, heading toward the two buildings she and Brock had targeted as possible hideouts.

Dong passed the shoe store, but then disappeared between the two buildings. She swallowed hard, hoping Brock wasn't back there. Then again, she knew Brock could take Dong out without breaking a sweat.

She paused, wishing she knew for certain which building Dong was going into, but turned to head back to the coffee shop. Brock would check the shoe store; he'd know where Dong was headed.

It was good enough for her to know they were on the right track.

She had only taken a few steps when she felt someone coming up behind her. Half expecting Brock, she turned.

Dong was there, bringing a metal pipe down on her head. She instinctively raised her arm to block it, but it was her left arm. Explosive pain overwhelmed her, and she sank to her knees.

Then blacked out.

The next thing she knew, she was on a cold, hard floor. Pain still reverberated through her body. She knew this time her left arm was broken by the force of Dong's lead pipe, but she forced herself to push the discomfort aside.

She didn't open her eyes but remained as still as possible while straining to listen. Two male voices spoke in low tones, and it took her a minute to realize they weren't speaking Chinese, but English.

She frowned, trying to make out their words. Her head pounded in conjunction with her broken arm, making it difficult to concentrate.

It sounded like the male voices were discussing options for getting away.

Liana assumed Dong had taken her to the former café or shoe store, whichever one was being used as their hide-out. He wasn't a large man, but he must have carried her there.

Were the girls Brock had seen here too? If so, she didn't hear them talking.

She forced herself to relax. She needed to remain calm. Rhy and the rest of the tactical team would be there soon. She hated knowing Brock would wonder where she was, but she hoped he focused on rescuing the girls.

Liana accepted the very real possibility she would be killed before Brock and the rest of the team could get into position.

She wished she'd told Brock how much she loved him. How much she'd missed him.

How much she wanted a second chance to do better.

The conversation abruptly stopped, making her wonder what had happened. Then pain exploded along her left side as she was brutally kicked in the ribs with enough force to send her rolling across the floor.

More broken bones, she thought, fighting to stay conscious.

"Stop pretending," a voice said sharply. "We know you're awake."

She had been awake but was now hanging on by a thread. She gasped, and said, "You broke my ribs."

"That's the least of your concerns," the voice said in a snide tone. "Nothing compared to what awaits."

Yeah, that's what she was afraid of. She shouldn't have followed Dong. Shouldn't have turned her back on the two buildings.

She should have been smart enough to wait for Brock, the way he'd asked.

She let out a low moan. "What do you want?"

"You cost me a lot of time and trouble." She blinked as a face hovered over her. It took a moment for her injured brain to recognize Muchin. "Money you will work hard to repay, understand?"

She understood exactly what he meant. He'd force her into prostitution like the others. She cowered and shook her head, playing up her fear. It wasn't hard. She hated everything about the man who loomed over her. "No, please, no. I can help you. I promise I can help!"

"Where is the cop?" Muchin leaned close, his awful breath making her gag. "Skinner said he was with you."

Skinner? Was that Tattoo Guy? She wondered if he was nearby, too, or still guarding the girls. It didn't matter really. She just needed to stall for time. "I ditched him."

Muchin's fist connected with her face. More pain exploded along her jaw, sending stars dancing in her line of vision. "Liar."

Liana couldn't stop the tears from streaming down her face. Every moment was agony. She silently begged for the strength she needed to withstand this. Brock would find her. He and the rest of the team would rescue them.

But if Muchin kept hitting and kicking her like this, there would be one less person for them to save.

She didn't think she could survive much more.

She wanted to close her eyes, but feared he'd kick her

again. Not that seeing the blow coming made it any less painful. She forced herself to meet his gaze. "Okay, I will tell you where he is. I just need to get up off the floor."

His hand came toward her again, making her recoil. But then he simply grabbed her arm and lifted her up and tossed her onto a hard chair. Even that much movement made her head spin with pain, but she gripped the edge of the seat with her good hand to keep from toppling over.

Her weapon was gone, as were the flashlight and binoculars she'd had. There was no time for regrets, though. Every minute counted.

"What are you doing?" another male voice asked from behind her. "You shouldn't have brought her here."

She turned to see who was behind her but then froze when Muchin's hand tightened painfully on her shoulder. "Don't move," he warned.

"Don't look at me, understand?" the other voice said. "Or you will die."

Was that Twisted Snake? The man she'd been hunting for months? She thought there may have been a hint of an accent in his voice, which had her leaning toward him being Twisted Snake.

"Dong found her lurking outside." Muchin's fingers didn't relinquish their grip on her shoulder.

"Where's the cop?" the voice asked.

"I sent Dong to find him." Manchin shrugged. "However, if he is nearby, we need to move."

The voice let out a stream of curses at the suggestion. "I'm tired of moving and being found. We must eliminate the threat once and for all."

"Agree." Muchin's fingers tightened. "We can start with this one."

"I know where the cop is hiding out," she said. How

much longer could she keep them from killing her? "He's at the coffee shop. The one on the corner."

A door burst open. She didn't dare move her head for fear Muchin would hit her again. Or simply pull his gun to kill her.

"No sign of cop," a breathless man said. She felt certain the man speaking was Dong. "I looked everywhere. No cop," he repeated for emphasis.

Please don't pack us up to leave, she thought desperately. *We must stay here for a while longer.*

"Put her with the others." The unknown man sounded dismissive, as if he couldn't be bothered with her. "We may need to use them as hostages. She will be more valuable than the others."

Muchin finally released her. She swayed with relief. "Take her down to the women," he instructed Dong.

Thank You, Lord Jesus!

She waited for Dong to step into her line of vision. When he reached for her injured arm, she held it against her chest and slowly rose to her feet. She stood for a moment, willing her knees to stop shaking. Fear, adrenaline, and pain were wreaking havoc in her body.

"This way," Dong said without smiling.

She stepped forward, resisting the temptation to look back over her shoulder at the unknown man. Getting a good look at the man who could very well be Twisted Snake wasn't worth the risk of being hit again.

Besides, she was grateful to be taken to where the other women were being held. The good news was Brock knew how to get into the room via the secret passageway.

Was the rest of the tactical team already assembled at the Foxhound restaurant? Was that why Dong hadn't found Brock?

Dong opened a door and stood to the side. When she walked past, he gave her an extra push on her back. Without the steel pipe, he wasn't very strong, so she managed to stay on her feet. But then she saw Tattoo Guy leering at her.

What was his name? Skinner. She swallowed hard and tried to ignore him. Stepping farther into the room, she saw several women staring at her. As if they were upset she was there. She searched their faces for Mai Shi, but her left eye was swollen to the point it was partially closed, and she was having trouble seeing clearly.

No one said anything for a long thirty seconds. She was about to lower herself to the floor beside two other girls, when one of them said, "She looks just as bad as the other guy."

"That's what you get for being a troublemaker," another girl groused. "Now we'll all suffer."

Liana understood they were in survival mode. There was no reason to take their comments personally. They'd be upset no matter who had angered the heartless thugs holding them hostage.

"What other guy?" she asked with a frown. She wondered if Yuze and Lin had been taken hostage too. It would explain why the BOLO hadn't yielded any results.

"Him." One of the girls waved to the corner. "Another troublemaker, like you."

Shifting her gaze to the corner, she frowned when she saw a badly beaten and bloody man. His head lolled to the side, and from here, he appeared unconscious.

She took a step toward him, but Skinner barked out a simple command. "No. Stay with the women."

"Yeah. Sure." She gingerly lowered herself to the floor, her broken ribs screaming in pain. But there was something familiar about the man slumped in the corner. He wasn't Chinese.

Straining to focus with her good eye, recognition slowly dawned. The badly beaten man was her handler, Lieutenant Troy Wallace.

CHAPTER THIRTEEN

Liana was gone. Brock had returned to the corner coffee shop to discover she wasn't waiting for him as arranged. He searched the area, returning to the street that ran along the front of the abandoned buildings. There were scuff marks in the snow on the sidewalk, making him think she'd been captured by the sex traffickers.

His first instinct was to head back to Lu Chen's to use the tunnel to save her. But he forced himself to turn away, leaving the street so as not to garner attention. He needed to wait for backup. He couldn't free the women being held there by himself. Not with what was likely several armed guards inside.

He called Rhy. "Where are you?"

"At the Foxhound restaurant. Where are you?" Rhy asked impatiently. "Liana told us to use this place as our center of operations. I have Jina stationed on the rooftop now, sighting our target."

"Great. Liana is there with you, then." Brock relaxed, realizing he shouldn't have assumed the worst.

"No, she's not. I thought she was with you?"

His heart sank. His initial fear had proven correct. "No. I think they have her." He wanted to kick himself for leaving Liana there alone. He forced himself to focus on their next steps. "Where's the Foxhound?"

Rhy gave him the address. He found the place without difficultly. Liana had chosen well. From street level, he couldn't see their sharpshooter, Jina. Steele was another sharpshooter for the team, too, but he was out on paternity leave now that Harper had given birth to a beautiful baby girl they'd named Amelia.

Inside the restaurant, a female manager looked upset. "I can't just shut the place down for business," she insisted.

"Yes, you can. This is important." Rhy was being polite but firm. "Lives are at risk. Young women's lives," he added for emphasis. "We need your cooperation on this."

"How am I going to explain this to the owner?" she asked.

"I'll talk to the owner. Right now, we need all the people here to leave," Rhy said. "Please. The sooner we get set up, the sooner we'll be out of your hair."

"Okay, okay." The manager hurried off.

Brock raised a brow, and Rhy shrugged. "It'll be fine. Are you sure Liana is being held inside?"

"I believe so. She isn't at our designated meeting spot." He glanced at Raelyn and Grayson who were standing nearby. "I'm hoping one of you will come with me through the tunnel."

"Hold on." Rhy lifted a hand. "We need intel and a plan."

"I know." He forced himself to think rationally. "There's obviously the front door and a rear door. We also have the tunnel access."

"How many gunmen?" Rhy asked.

"Unknown. One for sure, at least two others." He swallowed hard, thinking about Liana being inside. "They likely have Liana's weapon too."

"How many victims that can be used as hostages?" Grayson asked.

He sighed. "That's unknown too. I caught a glimpse of at least five, but there could be more. I had to back out as soon as I saw the tattooed gunman. I didn't want him to know we'd found the tunnel. And I was afraid he'd recognize me from when he took shots at us from Liana's apartment window."

Raelyn and Grayson exchanged a look. No doubt wondering about the rest of the story. But there wasn't time to rehash that now.

"Can Jina see into the building?" he asked.

"Let's go up and talk to her." Rhy led the way up the stairs to the rooftop. The place was nice, or would have been in warmer weather. The stiff breeze off the lake chilled to the bone.

Jina was crouched in her sniper's nest on the side of the building that offered a direct line of sight to the abandoned café. She had her rifle set up on a tripod and was peering through the scope.

"Can you see anyone inside?" Rhy asked as they approached.

She continued looking through the scope. "The windows are dirty, so it's not easy. I can see shapes, but it's hard to know if they are armed or possible victims."

Brock's stomach tightened. This wasn't good. It would be difficult to breach the building without knowing what they were facing inside.

"Anyone on the second floor?" Rhy pressed.

"I wish," Jina muttered. "Those windows are easier to

see into. I did get a glimpse of one man, but that was roughly five minutes ago. I haven't seen him since. I've been focused on the main floor where there are people moving around."

"The tunnel from Lu Chen's runs under the parking lot over there." He gestured with one hand. "There are steps down from the kitchen cooler, then a straight shot across, but then only a couple of steps go up on the other side. It's hard to know if the women are being held on the main level or in the basement. If there is one," he added.

"Gabe is getting us a blueprint of the building," Rhy said. He lifted his phone. "Should be coming in any minute."

A blueprint would be helpful, but he still wanted to know how many armed intruders were inside.

"What about a drone?" He turned to Rhy. "Could that help?"

"I've thought of that, but if the windows are covered in grime, I'm not sure a drone gives us an advantage." Rhy shrugged. "Jina can barely see through the windows, so I think we're stuck with what we have."

"There's one area of the window that isn't as bad as the others." Jina kept her eye pressed to the end of the scope. "Give me some time. I'm getting the impression they're moving around a bit as if restless. I just saw one man go past. I didn't see a gun, but I think we can assume any men inside are armed. I may get a glimpse of another soon."

Brock knew he needed to be patient. To trust his team to do the job they've been trained to perform. But imagining what Liana was going through at the hands of these ruthless men was ripping him up inside.

For all they knew, she could already be dead.

Please, Lord Jesus, keep Liana and the other women safe in Your care!

The prayer helped bring a sense of calm to his ragged nerves. Liana was strong. She would hang on until they could get there.

Rhy clapped him on the shoulder. "Let's head back down to the main restaurant. Zeke, Joe, and Cassidy have just arrived." He lifted his phone. "Flynn and Roscoe are five minutes out."

Roscoe Jones was the newest member of their team, a transplant from Texas. He followed Rhy downstairs. He felt better knowing all hands would be on deck for this situation.

Especially with Liana's life on the line.

"Are you okay?" Cassidy asked, when the team gathered around. She, Jina, and Raelyn were the three female cops on the team. Good at their jobs and sometimes more astute than the rest of the guys gave them credit for.

Not really, but he nodded anyway. "Yes." He turned to Rhy. "I think we need to break into three teams. One group goes in the back, one the front, and I'll take someone with me through the tunnel. We'll breach on my command."

Rhy arched a brow. "Not on your command. I think it's better for Jina to make the call. I'll have Joe go up to act as her spotter. You have verified for us that there are innocent women inside being held by at least one gunman. Once Jina eliminates one threat, the rest of the team members can breach the building." Rhy held Brock's gaze for a moment. "Your job from within the tunnel is to take care of the gunmen while getting as many innocent victims out as possible. Understand?"

"Of course." He glanced at Raelyn. She stepped closer as if silently agreeing to back him up in the tunnel. With unspoken agreement, they'd acknowledged their job would be to get the girls out while also searching relentlessly for Liana.

A few minutes later, Flynn and Roscoe joined them.

"Okay, here's the plan. Flynn, you and Roscoe will take up a position on either end of the street to grab any runners." Rhy doled out assignments. "Grayson and Cassidy will take the back door. Zeke, you and I will take the front." Rhy's gaze landed on him. "Brock and Raelyn will cover the tunnel. Jina and Joe will be on the roof as our sniper and oversight." Their boss scanned the group of faces. "Any questions?"

"Just one, Cap," Roscoe drawled in his Texas accent. "The runners could go out the back too. If y'all don't mind, I think Flynn should stay out front while I cover the back."

Rhy nodded slowly. "Good idea. Anything else?"

"No, sir," the rest responded. Brock nodded, anxious to get started.

"Hang on." Rhy held up his hand when his phone pinged. He glanced at his text, then quickly sent the message to the rest of them. "Gabe Melrose just sent the blueprint." Rhy's gaze held Brock's. "There is a basement."

That figured. But the news also didn't change the plan that much. Except now he wondered if the girls were being held in the basement rather than on the first floor. "Okay, we'll obviously know more once we get inside. If the tunnel leads into the basement, then the team coming in through the front should sweep the upstairs too. The team going in through the back might want to head down to the basement."

"Agreed." Rhy waited until the others nodded. "Ready? We'll get into position but hold fast until Joe gives the signal and Jina takes the shot."

Brock nodded. "Raelyn and I will need a ten-minute head start to get into the tunnel."

"Go." Rhy nodded. "We'll wait until you're in place."

Brock couldn't wait to get out of there. He desperately wanted to get back to the tunnel where he would be one step closer to Liana.

Stay strong, he silently told her. *Get ready. We're coming for you.*

And prayed she'd still be alive when they arrived.

LIANA BATTLED WAVES OF PAIN, especially in her head and arm, while doing her best not to antagonize Skinner, a.k.a. Tattoo Guy. It wasn't easy since he continued staring at her as if he couldn't wait to get his hands on her. She wasn't sure if his goal was to beat her some more. Or sexually assault her. Likely both.

Glancing at the prone figure of Troy Wallace, she tried to ascertain if he was still breathing while wondering what had happened. How had Troy gotten here? Had Brock been right about Troy working for Twisted Snake? If so, why was he down here, suffering from a horrible beating? Because he'd failed in his mission? Bai was dead and so was Xiong. It made sense that Muchin and Twisted Snake would do the same to Troy.

The girls around her had fallen silent, too, as if they weren't willing to talk while in the presence of a troublemaker.

Wasn't that what they'd called Troy? A troublemaker? That seemed to indicate Troy wasn't a part of the sex trafficking.

That maybe he'd come searching for her on his own after she and Brock had cut off all communication with him.

She told herself it didn't matter since Troy was obviously no longer a threat. She just needed to hang on long enough for Rhy, Brock, and the rest of the team to breach the building. Doing so would likely result in casualties. Unless she could figure out a way to disarm Skinner over there.

When she did glance in his direction, she sometimes saw two of him. Closing her left eye helped bring the man into focus. Her headache didn't make it easy to concentrate, either, although all she needed was to keep an eye, her good eye, on the man with the gun.

"You just wait," Skinner said with a humorless smile that made her feel sick to her stomach. "Your turn is coming."

She averted her gaze, suppressing a shiver. Apparently, he wanted revenge for the way she and Brock had gotten away. She told herself not to think about it. The bigger question here was what they were waiting for? She had to assume the goal was to get these girls out of there as soon as possible, moving them to a new location.

Or maybe they were waiting for someone important to show up. It could be that the man who'd spoken from behind her wasn't Twisted Snake, the way she'd assumed. Muchin and Skinner were the only two she knew by sight.

Who was Twisted Snake? And more importantly, where was he? She desperately hoped either Muchin or Skinner would lead them to the man in charge.

Troy let out a low moan. She glanced at him, glad he was still alive. Then she looked away, unwilling to let on that she knew him.

"What did he do?" she asked.

"None of your business." Skinner didn't take the bait. "Nosy people end up dead."

She shrugged as if she didn't care one way or the other. "Whatever. I don't care why you're keeping him around."

Troy moaned again and shifted. His face was battered, too, and she wasn't sure he was in any shape to see her, much less recognize her. She hoped that if he wasn't a part of this, he'd stay down until Brock and his teammates arrived.

If they arrived. She swallowed hard and tried not to show her despair. What was taking them so long?

"Go out there and search for him again!" Raised voices reached her ears. She couldn't help glancing upward toward the sound. While muffled, she was still able to understand what was being said. "We need that cop!"

"He's gone," a whiny Chinese voice said. "I search everywhere, the way you tell me to. He's gone!"

She felt certain the voice belonged to Dong and was secretly glad he hadn't found Brock. After showing her the way down here, it sounded as if Dong was now in trouble over his failure too.

Good. She hid a smile of satisfaction, hopeful that Dong's inability to find Brock was because he was at the Foxhound restaurant with Rhy and his teammates, who were hopefully right now coming up with a plan to get them out of there.

Her good eye adjusted to the dim lighting, making her frown when she realized they were in a basement. A fact she hadn't realized earlier. No wonder the voices from up above were so faint. The tunnel from Lu Chen's was deceiving, since it started on the main level, then went down and came back up.

But not all the way up to street level as she'd originally thought.

Did Brock know they were in a basement? She wasn't sure. Where was the doorway he'd looked through anyway? Without being too obvious about it, she turned just a bit in an effort to find the door. Her broken ribs zinged with pain at the movement, forcing her to stop lest she pass out again.

Red dots swirled in front of her eyes for a moment before they cleared. Okay, no more twisting or turning. She had to assume the door leading to the tunnel was behind her. And it made sense, as that was the easiest way to get the girls out of there.

And Brock had mentioned seeing both the girls and the armed Tattoo Guy.

Without warning, a muffled gunshot came from up above. A horrifying silence cloaked those of them in the basement.

Even though she couldn't see what was happening, she knew Dong had been shot with a pillow or something else used as a silencer. Killed for failing in his mission to find Brock. Her gaze darted to Skinner, who looked a little shocked too.

Was she next?

There was a scuffle from above, then another prolonged silence. She could almost imagine Dong's body being carried away and dumped in another room like garbage. Dong had attacked her, breaking her arm with the pipe, then carrying her there, feeding her directly into the lion's den.

Yet she still felt bad about his murder.

It only proved how Muchin and whoever else he was working for were cruel and ruthless.

And she hoped and prayed that even if she died here

today, that Brock, Rhy, and the rest of the tactical team would find and arrest Muchin, Skinner, and whoever else was involved.

Please, Lord, don't allow my death to be in vain. Please guide Brock and the others so they may save these girls!

As she sat on the floor, isolated to a certain extent from the girls gathered beside her, she thought about her role in their escape. She might be injured, but she was still a cop and needed to do something when the opportunity presented.

She eyed the distance between her location and Skinner. At least ten feet spanned the width between them. Far enough that he was out of reach, but close enough that he could shoot her. It wouldn't be easy, given her current condition, but the moment she heard the team breaking in, she would throw herself at Skinner, drawing his attention and making herself a target.

It would be worth it to save the girls from living this life of horror. Her only regret in her plan to sacrifice herself was not having the chance to tell Brock how much she loved him.

How much she wished they'd had more time together. To love and cherish each other.

That if given the chance, she'd marry him all over again.

Tears pricked her eyes, but she blinked them away. This wasn't the time for sentiment. She needed to be prepared, to be ready for action.

The voices upstairs grew louder. Two men arguing. Muchin and who? Twisted Snake?

Then she heard the sound of breaking glass followed by a thud. This was it! She pushed herself to her feet, intending to run toward Skinner, when gunfire came from somewhere behind her.

The tunnel?

The girls screamed and covered their heads with their hands. Liana dimly realized she had overestimated her ability to rush Tattoo Guy. Every muscle in her body screamed in agony when she moved. She'd barely taken one step when Skinner fell to the ground beneath the force of a bullet.

One down but several others to go.

"Liana!" Brock's shout filled her with joy.

"Here!" The word was garbled because of her swollen mouth. In addition to the broken arm and ribs, she wondered if her jaw was broken. She quickly turned toward the girls. "Go!" she shouted above their screaming and crying. And who could blame them for being afraid? "That way, hurry!" She pointed to the tunnel door. She tried desperately to speak clearly. "Escape to freedom!"

As if finally understanding, the girls jumped into action. Liana ignored Skinner's dead body, taking only a moment to reach down to grab his gun before turning toward the stairs. She needed to find the man known as Twisted Snake.

She could not let him slip away.

"Liana, this way!" Brock shouted.

She ignored him. Maybe it was because of the way Muchin had beat her, but she wasn't leaving until she found Twisted Snake. Without verifying for herself that he was the mastermind of this sex-trafficking operation.

Liana felt as if she was moving through molasses. She only made it up two steps when the door opened from above, and a stunning Chinese woman came rushing down. The fear in her eyes had Liana understanding she was another woman being held against her will.

"This way." Liana moved to the side so the woman

could come the rest of the way down. "Through the tunnel."

The Chinese woman grabbed Liana, twisting the gun from her uninjured hand before she understood what was happening. Then she hauled Liana close, pressing the barrel of the gun to her temple. "Back off or I'll kill her."

What? Who was this woman? Liana mentally chastised herself for being so foolish as to believe she was another victim.

"Drop the gun." Brock's calm voice wafted through the space between them. He sounded as if he only wanted to have a calm and rational conversation with this woman, despite the weapon he held in two hands pointed directly toward them. "There's no way out. Killing her won't save you."

"We're leaving right now!" The woman's harsh voice spat near her ear. "Toss the gun and step aside. I know how much you care about her."

How did this woman know that? Liana didn't understand who was holding her at gunpoint or what her role was within the operation.

Brock's gaze remained centered on the woman. "It's over," he repeated. "And you have a chance to save yourself by letting her go."

"Never," the woman hissed. "Don't try that negotiation bull with me. I'm safe while I have this cop as my hostage."

Wait, the woman holding her knew Liana was a cop? And that Brock cared about her? She glanced to where Troy was lying in the corner, a resigned expression in his eyes. Was it possible he knew who this woman was? If so, she wished he'd clue her in.

Unless . . . a sudden stillness washed over her.

The woman holding her hostage was Twisted Snake.

CHAPTER FOURTEEN

Brock held the Asian woman's gaze as he edged farther into the room. His heart thudded painfully in his chest, and sweat ran in rivulets down his spine. He was known to be the best hostage negotiator of the team, but in this moment, he felt like a fraud.

Just seeing the bruises marring Liana's face made him livid. Who had done that to her? If it had been the work of Tattoo Guy, he'd had gotten what he deserved.

With an effort, he strove to remain calm, the muzzle of his weapon pointed at the Asian. "You can survive this," he said again, "but only if you let Liana go." It had knocked him off kilter that this woman seemed to know who he and Liana were. Not just their professions as cops, but as husband and wife. "If you kill her, I'll have to kill you."

"You won't kill me," the woman sneered. "I know how this works. Step to the side and let us through. And call your fellow cops to let us pass by too. I'm sure you're not here alone. Once we're safely away from here, I'll let her go."

Brock knew that was a lie; although to her credit, the

Asian woman didn't look away from him. Most liars couldn't hold their gaze steady. But this woman could.

"Go ahead, Brock, let us go," Liana said in a choked voice. "There's no sense in keeping us here." She seemed to be trying to tell him something with her gaze, but he wasn't getting the message. Maybe because her left eye was puffy and nearly swollen shut.

"That's not going to happen." He kept his voice calm and soothing, the barrel of his weapon never wavering. "The gig is up. We have the place surrounded. There's nowhere for you to go."

At that, the woman holding Liana tightened her grip, making Liana wince in pain. "Step aside, cop. I won't tell you again."

Was there a hint of movement from behind the Asian? Brock abruptly lifted his gun, pointing it to the ceiling and holding his other hand out toward her. "Okay, okay. You're right. We're not going to shoot you while you have Liana."

"Move!" the Asian woman barked. The command in her tone indicated she was used to being obeyed without question.

Was she in charge? Was this woman the elusive Twisted Snake? Liana had thought the big boss in charge was a man, but from here, he could see a hint of tattoos darkening the skin along the Asian woman's wrists.

"I'm moving. See?" He purposefully took a step to the side, exposing the tunnel behind them. Somehow, Raelyn had gotten the girls out of there. Now there was only a badly injured man in the corner of the room, the dead tattooed guy, and the Asian woman holding Liana. "If you want to go, that's fine. But I still think you're taking a risk."

"I live for risk," the Asian woman said. "Keep going. Join your fellow officer Troy over there in the corner."

Troy Wallace? Brock didn't dare take his gaze from the Asian woman holding Liana to verify the guy's identity. He took another step to the side, hoping she didn't realize he was also moving forward.

There had to be a way to convince this woman to give up before anyone else died here today.

Whoever was behind the Asian moved again.

"Stop!" The Asian abruptly pulled the gun from Liana's temple and fired indiscriminately over her shoulder at whoever was behind her. Then she fired toward him, sending him darting to the side. Liana broke away, then crumpled into a heap on the floor.

The Asian woman screamed obscenities as she continued firing the weapon while darting toward the tunnel. Brock managed to get himself back on track long enough to aim and fire at her.

She disappeared around the edge of the door.

"Don't let her escape," Liana croaked.

He wanted to run toward Liana but forced himself to follow the Asian woman instead. It was what he'd do if it were Grayson or one of the other guys who were down on the ground and temporarily incapacitated.

But he couldn't get the image of Liana's bruised face from his mind.

The Asian was moving fast, taking the occasional shot at someone up ahead. He silently prayed for Raelyn and the girls to stay well out of the woman's way.

"No!" A scream rent the air. Brock quickened his pace, keeping his weapon trained on where the Asian had last been.

When he came to the stairs leading up into the cooler of Lu Chen's, he paused, mounting them cautiously, braced for the sudden impact of a bullet.

But when he reached the top of the stairs, there was no sign of the Asian. Using his elbow, he carefully pushed the long hanging plastic aside, peering through the cooler into the kitchen.

Only to find the cooler door was closed.

Rushing forward, he tried to open it. But it must have been locked from the outside. He reached up for his radio. "Rae? Are you there?"

There was nothing but silence in response.

Had the Asian grabbed another cop? He called Rhy. "Liana is safe, but Raelyn isn't answering. She could be with a tall, skinny Asian woman suspected to be Twisted Snake. She's armed and dangerous."

"We'll fan out and search the place," Rhy responded. "I've put Jina and Joe on alert too. If they find them, she'll do what she does best."

"Good." He spun away, quickly retracing his steps back through the tunnel to reach Liana. When he got there, he found Grayson kneeling beside her.

"Easy now, let's get you upright," his teammate was saying.

"I lost the Asian." He crossed over to join them. "Rhy is asking the team to fan out to search for her. The Asian may have Raelyn."

Grayson's expression turned grim. "Okay, but who is this Asian woman we're looking for anyway?"

"Twisted Snake," Liana said. "At least, that's what I believe."

"Got it." Grayson turned and bolted back up the stairs to the main level. Brock knew his teammates had likely cleared the building.

He'd been the only one to fail in capturing the woman.

"Her name is Ginji." A hoarse male voice caught

Brock's attention. With a frown, he glanced over to where a man lay half propped in the corner of the basement. He narrowed his gaze, pegging the injured man to be a white guy, maybe in his midforties.

"You're Troy Wallace?" He raked his gaze over the man's bloodied clothes. "Are you one of them?"

"No." The guy coughed, a pained expression crossing his features as he clutched his chest. "I was working with Liana."

"He's hurt." Liana was sitting on the bottom step, holding her side.

He inwardly winced at how much older Troy was than he'd imagined. Or maybe he just looked older because of the swelling and bruises. He turned back to Liana. "How do you know he's not involved? I heard they found Dong upstairs dead from a gunshot wound to the back of his head, shot execution style. Seems to me Wallace could have been working with them too. They could have beat him up because he failed to bring you in."

"I'm not involved." Wallace grimaced. "I was searching for you and Liana. I was afraid you were dead."

Yeah, he wasn't convinced of Troy's innocence. At least as far as the sex-trafficking organization went.

"I heard them kill Dong," Liana said. "He had been sent to find you, Brock. But he couldn't."

That was news to him. Still, he wasn't about to let Wallace off the hook. He turned back to the cop. "You expect us to believe you just stumbled into the sex-trafficker's hideout? One we found purely by accident coming through the tunnel from Lu Chen's?"

"Tunnel?" Wallace looked confused. "What tunnel?"

"There's a tunnel between Lu Chen's and this building," Liana said, her gaze sympathetic. "Try not to worry about it. We'll get an ambulance here soon. We can talk later, okay?"

Once again, Liana was defending the guy. He strove for patience. "She's right about the ambulance. We'll get them here ASAP. Let's get you upstairs, Liana. Then I'll come back for Wallace."

"I can walk," she protested.

He ignored her. When he wrapped his arm around her waist, she sucked in a harsh breath. "Broken ribs," she whispered.

Not just her ribs, he realized. Her left arm and maybe her jaw too. He loosened his grip and stepped back, feeling helpless. "Who did this to you?"

"Dong broke my arm. Muchin did the rest, although there was another man too." She grimaced, bracing her good arm on the wall. "I thought he was Twisted Snake. It never occurred to me that the leader was a woman."

A woman who was on the loose. Possibly with Raelyn. He tried not to think about the possible outcome his teammate faced.

"Take your time," he advised Liana as she began walking up the stairs. "I'm right behind you."

"Help Troy up, too, please?" She took another step. "Even if he is involved, we can't leave him down here."

She was right. The guy needed medical attention as much as she did. He nodded. "Once you're upstairs."

"I'll make it on my own," Wallace said testily. "And to answer your question, the big guy with the tattoos found me at Liana's apartment. He's the one who beat me up and brought me here. He wanted me to call you, Liana. And I did, but you didn't answer."

The part about Tattoo Guy finding Wallace at Liana's apartment was plausible. But Brock was reserving judgment until he had all the facts. He carefully followed Liana up the stairs, ready to brace her if she fell, knowing he had no right to continue holding a grudge against Wallace.

Liana had agreed to this undercover operation. And looking at her now, he hated the toll it had taken on her.

It was only through God's grace that she was alive. That the Asian woman or any of the others hadn't simply killed her and moved on.

He bowed his head for a moment, silently thanking God for keeping her safe. Then added another silent prayer for Raelyn to be found unharmed too.

Shuffling movement from behind him indicated Wallace had managed to stand up and walk toward the stairs under his own power. He had to admire the guy's sheer grit and determination.

Liana was near the top of the stairs now, leaning against the wall for a moment. Then she took the last step to reach the main floor.

He was right behind her when the sharp crack of gunfire caught his attention.

No! Not Raelyn!

Liana must have had the same fear because she rushed forward. He quickly did the same, but the dirty and boarded-up windows hampered his vision. Brushing past Liana, who stood in the center of the room as if dazed, he ran toward the open and busted front door, the one Zeke and Rhy had breached.

"Got her," a male voice shouted.

"Who?" He swept his gaze over the scene outside. The Asian woman was lying on the ground, bleeding. Roscoe, who was supposed to be covering the back of the building for runners, stood over her.

The Texas transplant smiled grimly. "I had a clear shot, so I took it."

"Thanks, Roscoe," Raelyn said. She sighed and shook her head. "My fault. I shouldn't have let her get the drop on me."

"She got away from me first," Brock said. He crossed to the Asian woman and felt for a pulse. Nothing. She was dead. He rose to his feet, glancing around. "Where are the girls?"

"Flynn has them gathered in Lu Chen's," Grayson said.

He bent again and pushed up the sleeves of the Asian woman's jacket.

Tattoos of snakes twisting around her slender arms peered up at him. He looked up to see Liana coming toward him, her gaze zeroed in on the woman's arms.

"She really was Twisted Snake," she said.

"Yeah." He rose to his feet and went over to take her uninjured hand. "But she'll never hurt anyone ever again."

"I'm glad." Liana leaned against him. "Very glad."

So was he. He was aware of Rhy speaking into his radio and other team members gathering around as well. It appeared as if the immediate danger was over.

But he wouldn't rest easy until Liana had gotten some badly needed medical care.

And they were able to verify that her contact, Lieutenant Troy Wallace, wasn't involved in this scheme.

LIANA PUSHED through the pain to focus on Twisted Snake, also known, according to Troy, as Ginji. The woman didn't look dangerous now. It was too bad it had come to this, but Liana couldn't garner much sympathy for the woman. That any female could lure girls into sex trafficking was beyond reason.

Sure, Ginji likely had a similar story, but that should have convinced the woman to go straight. Not join the criminal organization.

Or worse, move up the ladder to lead the criminal organization.

She straightened, moving away from Brock to peer closer at the woman who'd nearly killed her. "She's older than I thought." She glanced up at Brock. "Early to mid forties?"

"Yeah, that looks about right. Not that it matters." He reached for her hand. "Rhy has two ambulances on the way."

"I heard." She tried to smile, but the left side of her mouth didn't move. She gingerly felt her face. It felt like a balloon. "Troy needs it more than I do."

"You're not standing where I am," Brock said with a dark frown. "You look as bad if not worse than he does."

That wasn't true. Troy had been unconscious much longer than she had. "Where are the girls from the basement?" It shamed her to realize she'd momentarily forgotten about them. "I need to see if Mai Shi is with them."

"She was," Troy said, limping toward them. "But be prepared, Liana. All of those girls have become addicted to drugs. It's how they were controlled by those in charge."

Brock suddenly turned on Troy. "And how do you know Liana's cousin Mai Shi is with them?" He took a menacing step toward him. "You seem to know an awful lot about this organization for a cop."

"That is true," Troy said. He dropped his gaze to Ginji. Liana thought he looked regretful for a moment, as if he mourned the woman's passing. But that didn't make any sense if Ginji was Twisted Snake, the ultimate leader of the sex-trafficking operation. As if sensing her gaze, he looked away, then added, "I know Hua Wong. Mai Shi is her daughter."

"Yes," Liana said. "Hua Wong is my aunt, and Mai Shi is her daughter." She turned to Brock. "I told you the reason I took this case was that it was personal to me. I hated knowing my cousin was taken for this purpose. I had to do this to try to find her."

"Okay, but I'm still confused. Why does Troy know Hua Wong, your aunt?" Brock held Troy's gaze for a long moment. "Are you saying this is personal to you too? Is that it?"

Shock waves washed over her. Liana hadn't made that connection; although in hindsight, she should have. "Are you Mai Shi's father? Is that what you're saying?"

The ambulance sirens grew louder as two of them rolled up the street. She couldn't hear Troy's response over the sound, so she waited for the drivers to cut the sirens off before asking, "Well? Are you?"

"No." Troy met her gaze. One of his eyes was black and blue and mostly closed with the swelling too. "I'm sorry to tell you this, Liana, but Ginji is your mother."

"What?" She stumbled backward as if he'd punched her in the face. "No. That's impossible. You told me my mother was a victim of the sex-trafficking organization."

"She was." Troy's gaze was full of apology as he turned to look at Ginji. "She gave you up for adoption, which was admirable. But she didn't leave the life. Instead, she used her talent and determination to climb the ranks."

No, no! This couldn't be real. He was lying to her. Lying!

She turned and walked away, doubling over as pain

coursed through her. Not physical pain, although that still reverberated through her body with the slightest movement. But a deeply visceral wound from which she'd never heal.

Why, Lord, why?

The question echoed over and over in her mind, but there was no response. Not this time.

"Liana, please." Brock was there, trying to put his arm around her without hurting her bruised ribs. "Let's get you looked at. The paramedics are here, see?" He gestured toward two men, one blond, the other dark. "Let them examine you."

"No." She pulled away. "I need to see the girls. I want to talk to Mai Shi."

"Ma'am, my name is Colin Finnegan," the blond guy said. "And I really need to examine you for a possible head injury."

"Later." She turned and headed down the street in the direction of Lu Chen's. Wasn't that where Brock had mentioned the girls were being held?

She needed to see her cousin. To see how difficult of a road it would be for Mai Shi to get clean and return to a normal life.

Normal. What was normal? She couldn't begin to comprehend this recent turn of events. Her own mother had been the leader of the sex-trafficking organization who had forced her cousin into participating. Her stomach rolled, and it was all she could do to put one foot in front of the other, walking steadily when she wanted to throw up. When she stumbled, Brock was there, slipping his hand beneath her good elbow.

"I'm here," he said in a low voice. "I won't leave you again, Liana. Not now, not ever."

He should, she thought wearily. Her DNA was rotten. Warped. Her own mother . . .

She tripped again. Brock steadied her. She drew in a shallow breath because deep breathing made her feel as if she were being stabbed with a hot pitchfork, forcing herself to concentrate.

Mai Shi's situation was her fault. Maybe if she had been able to infiltrate the organization sooner. Maybe if she'd have known her mother was involved . . .

She abruptly stopped and looked at Brock. "If Troy knew Ginji was my mother, then he probably knew she was in charge. Why hadn't he said anything? Why had he sent me into this mess blind to that fact?"

"Good question." Brock used his radio to contact Rhy. "Take Lieutenant Troy Wallace into custody. He has some serious explaining to do regarding his inside knowledge as to what Twisted Snake was up to."

"Roger that," she heard Rhy reply. "Bring Liana back here, she needs medical attention."

"Not yet." She pushed forward. The distance between the two properties seemed ten times longer than it had when she and Brock had first found the tunnel. With each breath, the knife in her side seemed to slide deeper.

But she kept moving forward, her gaze locked on Lu Chen's. Local squads were there, as were other uniformed officers.

She hadn't noticed the additional police response until now. She told herself the danger was over. And that no matter what faced her inside the restaurant, she'd help Mai Shi get through it.

"Hold on." A uniformed cop held up his hand. "This is a crime scene."

"I'm Officer Liana Greer, and this is Officer Brock Greer. We need to talk to the women inside."

Brock pulled out his badge, then gestured at Liana. "She's been working undercover. No badge at the moment."

The cop gave her a sympathetic glance, no doubt taking in her bruises and swollen eye. He stepped aside and gestured for them to pass. "Okay, go ahead then."

"Thank you." She needed to cut down on the talking because that made her face hurt more than it already did. When they reached the front door, Brock reached past her to open it. She realized he'd come in this way earlier.

To rescue her.

She'd neglected to thank him for saving her life. She would have done it now, but stepping across the threshold, her gaze landed on the groups of girls huddled together.

And one young girl all alone, curled in the corner of a booth, shaking badly. From withdrawal? Fear?

Both?

She took in the girl's features with her good eye, then crossed over to her. "Mai Shi? Is that you?"

The girl lifted her tear-streaked face, her eyes red and puffy from crying. "Who are you?"

"Your cousin Liana." She lowered herself into the booth, trying not to wince. "We met a few years ago." Her fault they hadn't kept in touch. She'd wondered why her aunt hadn't been able to attend her and Brock's wedding. But she hadn't pushed it either.

Because she hadn't known. Dear Lord in heaven, she hadn't known! Looking back, it was easy to see how her aunt Hua hadn't wanted to be close to Liana.

Mai Shi stared at her for a moment, then looked away. "I don't remember."

"That's okay. I do." She wanted to reach out to the girl

but wasn't sure how Mai Shi would react to human touch. "I'm so sorry, Mai Shi. I'm sorry I didn't get here sooner."

"I want to go home." Mai Shi's eyes filled with tears. "I want my mama."

She turned to look up at Brock, who nodded. "We'll call her mother right away. She can meet us at the precinct."

"Precinct?" Mai Shi's eyes widened in horror. "No! I don't want the police. No police!"

"They just want to ask a few questions," Liana said in a soothing voice. "No one will hurt you. I promise."

"No police." Mai Shi sobbed.

Liana exchanged a worried glance with Brock. What was this about? Delayed reaction to being rescued by police? Watching as Brock had shot and killed Skinner?

"Okay, that's fine. You don't have to talk to the police." She ignored Brock's frown. She gave him a level look. Mai Shi was only sixteen, which meant she couldn't be questioned without her mother present anyway.

"Go away. I want my mama." Mai Shi curled in on herself as if she couldn't bear to be touched.

Liana refused to add to the girl's misery. She rose to her feet. "We'll make sure your mom comes here, Mai Shi. She'll meet you here."

Thankfully, Brock used his radio to make the call. She heard him talking to Rhy who agreed to contact Mai Shi's mother, Hua Wong.

Liana moved toward the door, the accusing looks from several of the girls cutting deep. This wasn't her fault but her mother's.

So why did she feel so guilty?

"Is Mai Shi underage?" Brock asked as they went back outside.

"Sixteen." She shook her head helplessly. "Many of the

girls are likely underage. You'll need to sift through that, allowing those with families to return home."

"We will. Right now, I'm more concerned about you." His brow was furrowed. "Please let Colin Finnegan examine you."

She couldn't put off the inevitable for much longer. Besides, there wasn't anything more she could do here. In fact, just the opposite.

Her presence was a liability as far as getting the girls to talk.

"Okay." She forced herself to move forward, even though her knees threatened to give out at any moment. The adrenaline that had carried her through the worst of the beating and the aftermath had faded.

As if sensing her weakness, Brock reached for his radio. "Rhy? Get your brother and the rig to Lu Chen's before Liana passes out."

"He's already on his way," Rhy answered.

Colin and the dark-haired paramedic were jogging toward her with a gurney between them. Within sixty seconds, they had her on the gurney. Her ribs screamed in pain as they ran with her back to the rig.

She closed her eyes, wishing things were different. How? She didn't know.

"Will she be okay?" Brock asked with concern.

"We need to get her to Trinity Medical Center ASAP," Colin answered.

"Wait!" a rough male voice called out. Liana managed to turn her head in time to see Troy stumbling toward her. She was confused because she thought he was already being cared for by the other paramedics. "Liana? Wait. There's one more thing you need to know."

She stared up at him with her right eye. The left one

was completely closed now. As far as she was concerned, he'd told her more than enough. That her own mother was Twisted Snake.

"You need medical attention," she managed. "We'll talk about the case later."

"I'm your father," Troy blurted. "Your biological father. And I'm sorry for everything I've done."

Her vision blurred, the pain in her side getting worse by the moment. Then for the second time in her life, everything went black.

CHAPTER FIFTEEN

"Get her to the hospital!" Brock stared at Colin Finnegan who had a stethoscope out and was listening to Liana's heart and lungs. "Hurry!"

Colin ignored him, listening intently before lifting his gaze to his. "Her lung sounds are decreased on the left. I need to check for a tension pneumothorax."

He had no idea what that was. "Do it." Brock hated feeling so helpless. He watched in shock as Colin and the other paramedic lifted Liana's shirt beneath her jacket, cleaned the bruised skin around her ribs, and stuck a needle into her chest. There was a faint hissing sound that—based on Colin's thankful expression—was apparently a good thing.

"That worked. Good. We relieved the pressure. Now we'll get her to Trinity Medical Center."

"What about him?" The second paramedic jerked his thumb toward Troy Wallace. The guy looked as if he was in as bad of shape as Liana was.

And he claimed he was Liana's father. Brock had trouble believing it, not that Troy had a reason to lie. But this wasn't the time to get into a long conversation about the guy's relationship with Liana's mother. He wanted Liana taken to the hospital ASAP.

"Troy, you need to get back to the ambulance crew." The cop held a higher rank, but he didn't care. "We'll talk later. I'm going to the hospital with Liana."

Colin arched a brow at his announcement but didn't argue.

"Okay. Take care of her." Troy turned and limped toward the ambulance crew. Brock waved, getting their attention, and the two paramedics crossed over to meet Troy halfway.

Once that was done, he waited for Colin and his partner to get Liana inside the rig. She opened her unbruised eye, looking surprised to see him hovering close. He did his best not to get in Colin's way.

"Where's Troy?" she asked.

"He's being transported to Trinity Medical too. Relax now, you're safe. It's over." Brock's voice was tight with emotion. He'd come so close to losing her today. To losing her forever. "I want you to concentrate on your health, okay?"

"He's my father," she whispered. "Why didn't he tell me sooner?"

He shook his head as Colin took her vital signs. His partner was driving them to the best level one trauma center the city had to offer. "I don't know, Liana. But you'll have plenty of time to ask questions later."

Her good eye closed, then popped open again. "How many bad guys did you take down?"

He frowned. "I'm not sure. I heard the team discussing the takedown through the radio, but I was focused on eliminating Tattoo Guy as a threat and getting you and the girls out of there."

"I need you to call Rhy. Ask him." She winced and shifted on the gurney. "There were two men on the main level. Muchin and another. Muchin hit me . . ." She swallowed hard. "And the other man told me not to turn around to look at him. He said if I turned to look at him, I would die. I assumed he was Twisted Snake. But now . . ." Her voice trailed off.

"Easy, try to rest," Colin interjected, giving Brock a stern look. "Your pulse is going far too fast."

"He's right. Relax now." Brock offered his best reassuring smile.

"No. Call Rhy." The familiar stubborn set to her features made him sigh. "We need to know that guy with Muchin didn't get away."

"Okay, I'll call. But only if you agree to rest." He pulled the disposable cell from his pocket and moved as far away as he could manage in the small space. He trusted Colin Finnegan, so it wasn't about not letting Colin overhear. No, he was more concerned about being in the way if Liana's condition took a turn for the worse.

"Rhy?" He plugged his other ear with his finger to hear better. "It's Brock. Do you know how many we have in custody?"

"None in custody," Rhy said. "Unfortunately, they're all dead."

That wasn't optimal, but since they'd eliminated Ginji, a.k.a. Twisted Snake, as an ongoing threat, he hoped the organization would fall apart. "Liana said there were two guys in the main level who roughed her up. One was Muchin, the other unknown."

"Hang on. I'll check. I know Jina took one guy out seconds before we breached the structure."

Brock waited, watching with concern as Colin started an IV and hung fluids. Then he turned his attention to Liana's injured arm. She cried out in pain when he touched it, and by the grim expression on Colin's face, he suspected the injury was worse than he'd originally thought.

"Liana, I'm giving you something for pain," Colin said. "I think your left arm is broken."

"I think it is too," she whispered. "I heard the bone crack when Dong hit me with the steel pipe."

It was wrong, but Brock was glad Dong was dead. He turned away as Liana cried out again when Colin palpated her arm.

He hated knowing how badly she was hurt. On top of her broken arm and her swollen and bruised face, Colin had been forced to stick a needle in her chest. How much more could Liana take?

After what seemed like forever, Rhy came back on the line. "Okay, we have two dead men on the main level, one Jina took out, the second smaller dead Chinese guy was found in another room. He was shot execution style, and none of our teammates took him out. Then we have the woman we believe is Twisted Snake. The only other man down is the tattoo guy you eliminated. That's all."

Brock's stomach knotted. "Liana heard them execute Dong. She believes Muchin is the one who killed him because he'd failed to find me. So Muchin, Dong, Tattoo Guy, and Ginji are dead, but that means we're missing someone. There were two men on the main level besides Dong."

"I'm not sure how that's possible," Rhy said. "How could he have gotten away?"

"I don't know. But Liana is convinced there's one more player. And I believe her. She knew Dong and would not have mistaken him for someone else. She said the second specifically told her not to turn around or she would die. At the time, she assumed he was Twisted Snake. But now we know he's not."

"Okay. We'll spread out and see what we can find. Maybe there's another secret passage in the house we don't know about. Seems to be the common theme in this area," Rhy added with a snort. "There must have been a big bootlegging operation taking place in those buildings back in the day."

"Thanks. Let me know if you find him." He stuffed his phone back into his pocket. Who was the third man? And why had he insisted that Liana not turn around to look at him? Obviously, he'd wanted his identity to be a secret.

The driver of the ambulance suddenly hit the brakes, hard. Brock slid into a shelf full of medical supplies. He steadied himself, then leaned forward. "What's going on?"

"There's some cop out here waving me down!" The ambulance driver sounded frustrated. "I have my lights on; he shouldn't try to stop me. What does he want?"

Cop? Brock lurched closer, peering through the windshield. Sure enough, there was a cop standing in front of his squad that he'd parked sideways across the road.

He didn't recognize the cop's features, but there were captain bars on his sleeve. And that's when Brock knew. This was Captain Jorge Marbury, Liana and Troy's boss.

He was in on this!

"Don't stop. Swerve around him. Keep going," Brock urged. "And lower the passenger window. Quickly!"

The driver did as he asked. As if realizing they weren't going to stop, the cop on the street pulled his weapon and aimed at the rig. But he was a second too late. Brock already had his weapon and didn't hesitate to fire through the open passenger window. The cop looked shocked and ducked, grabbing his arm.

Brock had hit him! But then he lost sight of the cop as the ambulance rig bounced up and over the curb, swerving as they rounded the parked squad to continue toward the interstate. After clearing the squad, the driver put on a burst of speed as if desperate to get to the hospital.

He reached for his radio. "All units, be on alert for a Captain Jorge Marbury. Last seen on Hanover Street. He just tried to shoot at the ambulance carrying Liana to the hospital. Repeat, Captain Jorge Marbury is involved, dressed in uniform and armed."

"Roger that. We're on the way." He recognized Grayson's voice over the radio.

"You shot a cop!" the driver exclaimed.

"A dirty cop." He didn't have proof, except for the fact that Marbury tried to stop their rig while taking a patient to the hospital, which was unheard of. He felt certain he was right about Jorge Marbury being a part of this. It explained why he didn't want Liana to turn around to see him.

And since he was dressed in uniform, Marbury could have left the property and mingled with the other officers on scene without attracting attention.

"Brock?" Liana's voice had him turning back to look at her. "What happened?"

He hesitated, not wanting to say too much. He glanced at Colin who shrugged. "I think we found the guy who hit you and told you not to turn around."

"Who was he?" She must not have heard him talking to the team via his radio. Colin had mentioned giving her pain meds.

"We'll talk about this after you've been given medical attention." He hesitated, then added, "I would like to have you listen to different voices when you're able, see if you can recognize the one you heard."

"Okay." Her eye closed. "So tired," she whispered.

He bowed his head, silently thanking God for sparing Liana's life. And praying that he was right about Marbury.

Because if he wasn't? There was no question he'd lose his job and his place on the tactical team for shooting a cop.

LIANA WENT in and out of consciousness, hearing muted voices in the background every time she tried to open her good eye. Finally, she gave up.

When she next awoke, some of the fogginess was still there. But the voices were clearer. She could actually make out words.

"Her surgery went well," a deep voice said. "She'll have those pins in place to stabilize her fractured bones for a while, though."

Pins? Surgery? Her arm. She turned to peer at her left arm. It looked like a robot arm, a metal bar connected by several pins poking out of a huge cast.

"Thank you. What about her ribs?" Brock asked.

"Two broken ribs, one had punctured her lung, but they should heal in time. We used a spinal block to help manage her pain. Her jaw is badly bruised but thankfully not broken."

That made sense. Liana had to admit, she could breathe easier now. Although she suspected that once the nerve block wore off, the pain would return in full force.

"I'm glad about that. How long will she be here?"

Brock's voice again. She lifted her gaze, surprised to realize she could see out of both eyes now, to find him standing off to the side speaking to a man wearing scrubs and a lab coat.

"A couple of days. We'll see how it goes." The surgeon was noncommittal. If Liana had her way, she'd get out of there sooner rather than later.

"Water," she croaked. Her throat was as dry as sandpaper.

"You're awake." Brock came closer, a hesitant smile creasing his features. "Here, take small sips." He raised a cup of water, carefully placing the straw in her mouth. She took several sips, thankful for the icy coldness.

"How long"—she blinked the fog from her mind—"have I been out?"

"Six hours," Brock said. "But a big chunk of that was your surgery and recovery."

She was shocked, but it made sense. "What did I miss?"

Brock's expression turned guarded. "There's no rush. You can help with the investigation when you're up to it."

She frowned. She knew him too well; there was clearly something he wasn't telling her. "Did you find everyone involved?"

"We believe so," he said. "But we'll need you to verify something when you're feeling better."

"Now." She struggled to sit up. Brock leaned over and moved the head of her bed higher by pushing a button on the side rail. She sighed and then reached for his hand. "Please, Brock. I want to know that we have everyone involved. That the danger is over for good."

He hesitated, then nodded. "Okay. Rhy has put a list of male voices together on a computer program. We need you to listen to them, then tell us which one you think was in the room with you and Muchin."

"I can do that." She let him go so he could grab the computer. He pulled a chair up close to her bed, then cued up the audio files.

"Ready?" he asked.

She took a moment to clear her mind. To think back to when she was being held in the chair. She silently replayed the brief conversation.

What are you doing? Why did you bring her here? Don't look at me, understand? Or you will die.

"Okay, I'm ready." She injected confidence in her tone.

The first voice came through the computer speakers. "Don't look at me."

"That's not him." She gestured with her uninjured hand. "Next one."

There was a pause, before another male voice said, "Don't look at me."

She grimaced. "No, sorry. That's not it either." A wave of doubt hit hard. Was she wrong? She'd been kicked and punched, maybe she couldn't remember who had spoken. Maybe she couldn't do this.

"Here's the next one," Brock said. He pushed another button.

"Don't look at me."

"That's him!" She grabbed Brock's arm. "That's the man who was behind me."

"You're sure?" Brock asked. "I'd like you to listen to the next three voices, too, okay?"

"Okay." She knew it was important for her to be able to say under oath that after listening to six voices, she'd identified the correct one.

"Don't look at me." *Too gruff*, she thought.

"Don't look at me." *Too nasal.*

"Don't look at me." *Too husky.*

"It's the third voice," she repeated.

"You're absolutely sure? Enough to testify under oath?" Brock pressed.

"I'm positive. That's him." She held his gaze. "Who is he?"

Brock nodded and smiled. "You nailed him, Liana. That's Captain Jorge Marbury. We have him in custody. And now that you've identified his voice, he'll go away for a long time."

She couldn't believe Captain Jorge Marbury was a part of this. "Did Troy know?" The minute she said Troy's name, she remembered his last words to her.

I'm your father. Your biological father, and I'm sorry for everything I've done.

"Troy says he didn't know, but he became suspicious when we were burned at the restaurant." Brock hesitated, then added, "Troy is a patient here too. He had some internal bleeding in his liver that required surgery. I know you'll want to see him at some point."

"I guess." She was still coming to grips with knowing Troy was her father and her mother was Twisted Snake. She could imagine how they'd met. If Troy was about forty-five, roughly the same age as her mother, he would have been nineteen when Liana had been born.

A kid who'd likely paid for her mother's services early in her role as a prostitute. That's why he'd apologized. She could understand why her mother had given her up for adoption too. Yet at some point, her mother had turned her experience into a criminal enterprise. Despite what her mother had suffered, she'd pulled other innocent women into the same horrible life. Why had her mother turned evil? She'd never know.

"You don't have to do anything now." Brock set the

computer aside, then cradled her hand in his. "You've been through a lot. I just want you to know I'm here for you, Liana."

"Thanks." She managed a wan smile. "I wouldn't be alive if not for you. I'm grateful for your persistence in finding me."

"I almost lost you." The words were low and agonizing. "I love you so much, Liana. I know I screwed up, and I'm sorry. I never ever should have accused you of cheating on me."

She'd been so angry at the time, but now she knew it wasn't just the text message from Troy that had sent Brock on that path. She'd been secretive about the undercover job Troy had wanted her to take. That secretive behavior had likely contributed to his believing she was cheating.

"I owe you an apology, Brock," she said. "I shouldn't have left you like that. I should have warned you I was getting involved in a new role at work." Tears pricked her eyes. "I took the job because I knew from my mother's sister that my own mother had been trafficked as a teenager. Then I learned her daughter was missing too. When Troy presented the possibility of going undercover to break up the sex-trafficking ring, I jumped at it." She tightened her grip on his hand. "But I shouldn't have put work above our marriage. Our love. That was wrong. So very wrong."

"I understand," Brock said. He bent to kiss her hand. "I wish I'd handled things differently too. I should have trusted in your love for me."

"It's not your fault. It's mine." She wanted to ask for a second chance but wasn't sure she deserved it. And really, no matter what she'd done, she needed Brock to trust her.

To be fair, she needed to trust him too.

"I love you, Liana." His words filled her with hope and joy. "I always have, and I always will."

"I don't deserve you," she whispered.

That made him smile. "I think that's my line. I don't deserve you, but I hope and pray you'll give our marriage another chance. Please, Liana. I promise I'll work on my trust issues."

"Me too," she agreed. "Because I love you, Brock. I missed you so much over these past few months. I can't count how many times I almost called you, begging for you to help me on this undercover operation."

"I wish you had," he whispered. "I would have dropped everything to be with you. Yet I can understand why Troy was worried about me being overprotective. I can't lie, that is my nature, especially when it comes to protecting someone I love."

"Does that mean you forgive him?" she asked.

He grimaced, then nodded. "Mostly. I still think he should have pulled both of us into the op at the very beginning, but I think he's suffered enough." He hesitated, then added, "And he's your father. I have to forgive him as he'll be a part of the family."

Her heart swelled with love. "Thank you for giving our marriage another chance. I promise, no more undercover operations for me." She frowned, glancing at her robotic arm. For the first time, she suddenly realized she might not be able to continue working in her chosen career.

"The surgeon was pretty positive about your chances of having a full recovery." As if reading her thoughts, Brock hastened to reassure her. "I know you'll work hard, Liana. If anyone can get over this, you can."

His faith was humbling. "I hope so. Right now, I look like something out of a freak show."

"Never." He leaned in to kiss her. She reached up with her good hand to pull him in closer, craving his touch. After a long moment, he lifted his head and smiled. "I'll be with you the whole time. Together, we can do anything."

She loved the sound of that. But before she could say anything else, someone knocked on her door.

"Yes?" She assumed either a doctor or nurse was there, but it was Rhy who stepped across the threshold. "Oh, hi, Rhy."

"Liana. Brock." Rhy's gaze zeroed in on Brock. "I don't suppose you had a chance to test Liana's memory."

"I did. She identified the third voice in the lineup as the man who'd been behind her, warning her not to turn around or she would die. We got him, boss." Brock grinned. "He'll go down for his role in this."

"Good news." Rhy smiled back. "You should know that David Kimball is a distant relative to Marbury. That's the second connection that will seal the guy's fate. Thanks, Liana. I'm glad you were able to identify him."

"Me too." Her smile faded. "I'm still shocked a cop at his level was involved, though."

"Nothing surprises me anymore," Rhy said on a sigh. "However, we plan on digging into Captain Jorge Marbury's background. I suspect he's been getting paid to look the other way."

"Yeah, but that's the part that's bugging me." Liana frowned. "If he was involved, why would he ask Troy to send me undercover?"

"We don't believe the idea originated with Marbury," Brock said. It was clear he and Rhy had already discussed this.

"That's true." Rhy waved a hand. "You may as well fill her in on the rest."

"Officers down in Ravenswood found the owners Yuze and Lin Lu Chen," Brock said. "They're claiming they know nothing about the sex-trafficking organization, but their phone records prove otherwise."

That was good news.

"We also need to interview Troy further, but it sounds as if he came up with the plan after learning about Mai Shi going missing." Brock held her hand again. "He chose you for the assignment because you speak Chinese and because he knew you'd have a personal stake in the outcome. From what we can tell, Marbury didn't know about the details of the operation until you were several weeks into it. And that's when he began to undermine your position in the organization."

Her eyes widened in shock. "So you think Bai Chow would have killed me even if you hadn't stepped into the kitchen?"

"I believe so, yes." Brock grimaced. "We can't prove it, obviously, since all the major players are dead. Well, except for Marbury himself."

"God sent you to me that night, didn't He?" She held Brock's gaze. "If you hadn't come back to the kitchen . . ."

"I do believe God brought us together that night," Brock agreed. "And it's a good thing you met with me at PK's too."

"Everything happens according to God's plan," Rhy said with a smile. "Guess I should head back to update the ADA on Liana's voice identification."

"This late?" Brock glanced at his watch. "It's going on eight o'clock at night."

"Yes, my cousin Maddy Sinclair is waiting to hear from me." He grinned. "It's not every day you get to indict a police captain. She's including Bax in on this, too, since Maddy is due to have her baby any day now."

Liana nodded, remembering now about the family connections the Finnegan family had with the DA's office. Bax had rented them a car because of that connection too. "There's one more thing, though," she said.

Rhy and Brock both looked at her. "What's that?" Brock asked.

"We need to know if there are other girls out there." She held Brock's gaze. "For me, it's more important to know we've rescued all of them rather than tossing the book at Marbury. I want those girls to be free."

There was a long silence as both Rhy and Brock digested this. "Yes, I agree," Rhy said. "I'll talk to Maddy and Bax, see if we can't talk to Marbury, leveraging information in exchange for a lighter sentence."

"I'm all in on that plan too," Brock said. "As long as Marbury loses his pension and never wears the uniform again."

"That goes without saying." Rhy nodded. "The crime scene tech found Marbury's fingerprints in the old café. With his connection to the house on Duckwood, and your voice identification, and the fingerprints, we're building a solid case against him. We're starting to interview the girls. I'm sure one or more of them will also be able to ID him."

Liana relaxed back against the pillow, suddenly exhausted. "Thanks. Both of you."

Rhy nodded and turned to leave. Brock remained at her side. She clutched his hand as if it were a lifeline.

"Rest, Liana. I'll be here when you wake up." He bent over to kiss her again. "Everything will work out, you'll see."

"I pray you're right." She sighed. "I love you, Brock. Thanks for being here."

"Always."

She allowed her eyes to close, giving in to the need to

rest. And somewhere in her mind, she heard the Bible phrase again.

Be still and know that I am God.

With Brock at her side, and God's love surrounding her, a welcoming sense of peace washed over her.

This was where she belonged.

EPILOGUE

Three weeks later . . .

Brock came home from work to find Liana sitting on the sofa in their condo with Troy Wallace. He paused, then came farther into the room.

"Hi, Brock." Troy looked nervous as he rose to shake Brock's hand. "I'm sorry to barge in on you two like this."

"You're welcome any time," Brock assured him. He reached for Liana who eagerly stepped into his arms for a kiss. She still had what she jokingly referred to as her robot arm, the pins sticking out from her cast, but thankfully, she was healing nicely from her other wounds.

Her ribs still hurt, and the bruises on her face had faded. He'd noticed she was moving much easier now. He watched her like a hawk, but she remained stubbornly independent. He loved her strength and determination.

Yet he wished she'd waited to have this conversation with her father when he could be there but didn't voice the thought.

These past three weeks had been spent repairing their marriage and rekindling their love. They'd attended church with the Finnegans too. He'd promised to love and trust her, and he did. If she wanted to meet with her father privately, that was her right.

"I just wanted to offer another apology for my role in all of this." Troy appeared nervous. "I honestly didn't realize Ginji was the infamous Twisted Snake until they caught me. To say I was shocked was an understatement."

"I can only imagine," Brock agreed. He and Liana sat on the sofa. "But you don't need to apologize when it was Marbury who was involved."

"I feel like I should have known that too," Troy said. He sighed and rubbed the back of his neck. The lieutenant looked skinny, having had two abdominal surgeries to combat the internal bleeding he'd suffered. Troy turned to Liana. "I'm glad you're doing better."

"You too." There was an awkwardness to the conversation. Liana and Troy had worked together for three years, only now their blood bond seemed to stand like a tall brick barrier between them.

Troy sighed. "Well, I've intruded enough. I just wanted you to know that I'm sorry and that I've put in a transfer to district two." He grimaced, and added, "When I'm able to get back to work, that is." He turned to leave.

"Wait." Liana stood. "I can't lie, it's going to take time to become accustomed to having a father, but I hope we can get together again. Maybe for Easter? I—you're welcome to attend church services with us." She sent Brock a teasing glance. "And Brock will cook, too, won't you? I can't do much with my left arm in a cast."

"Of course," he readily agreed.

A smile bloomed on Troy's thin face. "I'd like that. Very much."

"Good." Liana put her good arm around her father's

waist and gave him a quick hug. "We'll stay in touch too. Okay?"

"I'm glad you and Brock have each other," Troy said. He nodded thoughtfully. "Take care, both of you."

Brock followed Troy out of the condo, locking the newly repaired and reinforced door behind him. "Sounds like that went well," he said, turning back to Liana.

"It did." She hugged him again. "I heard from Rhy earlier too. They found all three locations Marbury had given them. They rescued twenty more girls."

"I'm glad." Rhy had already given him the news, but he was touched by the way his boss had reached out to Liana personally. After all, it was her case.

And they'd done good work, even though all the girls involved, including Mai Shi, had a tough road ahead of them.

He and Liana prayed for them every day.

"I had this crazy idea," Liana said, "about what to do with my life after my arm is healed."

"What's that?" He led her back to the sofa and pulled her onto his lap.

"Don't laugh at me, but I may want to go back to college." She glanced at him warily. "To study counseling."

"Counseling sounds perfect for you." He should have seen it coming, and he was thrilled with her decision. "I think that's a great idea, Liana. I'll support you in any way possible."

"I know you will." She kissed his cheek. "I'm more worried about my ability to be a good counselor. But I have to try. For the girls," she added. "As much as I loved being a cop, I can't just go back to working the street. I need to do more."

"I love you, Liana. I know you can do anything you set

your mind to." He caught her mouth in a deep kiss. Then lifted his head. "I have one more request, though."

"What's that?"

"I'd like to renew our marriage vows in our new church on our wedding anniversary, which I know is only three weeks away." It was an idea that had come to him when she was lying in that hospital bed.

"That's a great idea." She smiled widely. "I bet I can still fit into my wedding dress."

He laughed. "And I'll happily wear a tux." He turned serious. "I've learned from my mistakes, Liana. This time, I promise to do better."

"And I've learned from my mistakes too," she said. "There will always be struggles, Brock, that's what relationships are all about. But together, we can do anything."

"With God's love, all things are possible," he added.

I HOPE you enjoyed Brock and Liana's story in *Brock*. I've been having fun bringing love to each member of Rhy's tactical team. Are you ready for Raelyn and Isaiah's story in *Raelyn*? Click here!

DEAR READER

Thanks so much for reading my Oath of Honor series. I'm truly blessed to have wonderful readers like you. I hope you enjoyed Brock and Liana's story. I've been having so much fun bringing the Finnegans back into these books. What better way to keep track of what the family is up to? Joe and Elly are married, Kyleigh is pregnant, and Maddy is too. So much more to discover. You won't want to miss a single one.

Don't forget, you can purchase eBooks or audiobooks directly from my website, and you will receive a 15% discount by using the code **LauraScott15**.

I adore hearing from my readers! I can be found through my website at https://www.laurascottbooks.com, via Facebook at https://www.facebook.com/LauraScottBooks, Instagram at https://www.instagram.com/laurascottbooks/, and Twitter https://twitter.com/laurascottbooks. Also, take a moment to sign up for my monthly newsletter to learn about my new book releases! All subscribers receive a free novella not available for purchase on any platform. And this year, I've added a bonus epilogue for my newsletter subscribers describing Elly and Joe's wedding!

Until next time,
Laura Scott
PS: Read on for a sneak peek of *Raelyn*.

RAELYN

Prologue

Ten years earlier . . .

Isaiah Washington scanned the street for cops prior to approaching his drug contact, Petey Dobbs. Good thing the pigs didn't show up in this area very often. That made it easier to do business.

In this neighborhood, the Chief owned the streets. And the goal wasn't law and order but survival of the fittest.

"Yo," Petey said with a head bob. "Got what I need?"

"Got the cash?" Isaiah countered. Donte Wicks, his supplier, would want his money ASAP. The guy was as twitchy as the product he sold to those who lusted after it. Isaiah didn't much like being the middleman, but he hoped to have a face-to-face meeting with Donte's boss, the Chief, very soon. The more drugs he sold, the better his chances of moving up in the organization. This barely scraping by was getting old.

One good thing about selling dope: it was good and easy money.

Considering he and his ma were one step away from living on the street, that's all he cared about. He eyed Petey Dobbs warily. Petey was more skittish than usual. Isaiah wanted to make the sale and get out of there. Move on to the next job. With Donte, there was always another job waiting in the wings. And that was just fine with him.

"I'm a little short," Petey said, his gaze darting back and forth nervously. "But I'll get the rest by tomorrow. I promise."

"No cash, no deal." He was tired of Petey's games; this was the second time in a row the guy had tried to weasel out of paying. "Three hundred or nothing."

"Come on, Isa, you know I'm good for it," Petey whined. "My dad is out of town, but he'll be home later tonight. I promise I'll pay you in the morning."

Yeah, famous last words. Besides, he didn't believe him. No junky ever paid up after they'd scored their dope.

"No deal." Isaiah forced himself to turn away. There were others out there who would pay top dollar for what he had. He didn't need Petey as much as the idiot needed him. Finding a new buyer would take longer, though, and that delay would put Donte's undies in a wad. The guy had the patience of a cockroach.

"Okay, okay, wait!" Petey lunged forward to grab his arm.

Isaiah instantly reacted, lashing out with his fist and catching Petey in the jaw. He'd been robbed once before by a desperate junkie, and he wasn't about to go through that again.

Petey howled like a baby and let go of his arm. Isaiah took several steps backward, eyeing Petey cautiously. This was the second reason he didn't like being the middleman; these smack heads were unpredictable.

"Last chance." He should have left right away but had hoped Petey would hand over the cash.

Instead, the junkie whipped out a gun, pointed it at him, and pulled the trigger. The bullet slammed into his upper chest. The impact threw him off his feet, and he hit the ground hard, the back of his head bouncing off the pavement. Darkness hovered around the edges of his vision, but he did his best to stay conscious. He stared up in shock as Petey leaned over him and rummaged in his pocket for the drugs.

Then Petey was gone, leaving him lying in the street unable to move. He looked up at the faint stars in the dark sky. Waves of pain washed over him, and he could feel his strength ebbing away, his blood pooling in the street.

This was it. He was gonna die out here, like so many brothers had gone before him. This was why his teachers had insisted that crime didn't pay. Anyone who lived in the hood knew that being shot was always a risk. Nothing he could do about that.

Desperate times called for desperate actions. His mom's illness followed by losing her job had started him down this path.

One that would end here on a cold May night.

His biggest regret was not getting the cash his ma would need to stay in their rat trap of an apartment for another month. She needed him. Needed the money he brought home every week.

But he'd failed her.

He closed his eyes, wishing death would take him quickly. Suddenly a blindingly white light filled his field of vision. Was this a dream? Isaiah squinted against the brightness because it hurt his eyes. Was that a spotlight? Had the cops arrived? Turning his head carefully, he looked around, realizing he was still alone. There was nothing other than the dazzling bright light.

A strange sense of peace washed over him as his grandmother's voice reverberated through his mind.

Go to the light. Isaiah, you must go to the light!

To the light? Was the light heaven? He found himself transfixed by the warm brightness. Yet he also didn't understand why the light would shine for someone like him. He lifted his arm as if to touch the light and experienced the odd sensation of his body being lifted off the street, drawn upward into the light's embrace.

Warmth enveloped him, and his heart filled with hope. *Yes! I need the light! Please, Lord, take me to the light!*

Just the thought of seeing his grandmother made him smile. But then another deeper voice in his mind whispered, *Not yet. It's not your time, my child.*

Not yet? Or not ever? Isaiah closed his eyes, fearing the worst. That God had rejected him and was sending him straight to hell.

Where he belonged.

RAELYN

Chapter One

"Shots fired! Shots fired!" Lieutenant Joe Kingsley's voice was calm but tense in her earpiece. From her position at the abandoned warehouse, tactical police officer Raelyn Lewis could hear the shots easily enough; they sounded like firecrackers that might never stop. Her heart thudded painfully in her chest beneath her vest, but her hands didn't shake. She knew her job and was determined to execute it to the best of her ability.

She peeked out from behind the building to see what was happening. The situation outside the New Hope Church had spiraled out of control within seconds of the tactical team's arrival. The local police had gotten there first, and rather than dispersing, the group of kids had brandished their weapons and stood their ground.

It was like something out of a horror flick. Too many people with guns facing a slew of armed police officers. There was no way this would end well. The gunfire proved it.

More shots rang out, and even from here, she saw bodies crumpling to the ground. Not just those from the group of armed kids who'd started this mess, but there were at least three police officers down too.

Bad. This was really bad. The worst street riot she'd ever witnessed. And considering she'd grown up in a white-trash neighborhood in Chicago, that was saying something. Chicago had a worse gun-crime rate than Milwaukee, although you would never know it based on the scene unfolding today.

"We need to get the crowd under control," Joe said. "I want them surrounded. Jina, get in position."

"Roger that," Jina said.

"Moving in," Raelyn replied, agreeing with his command. The tactical team wasn't one for sitting around and watching. She quickly stepped out from behind the building. Her position near the abandoned warehouse happened to be the closest to the church. Grayson was on the other side of the church, and several of her other teammates were stationed in other areas. Jina, their sharpshooter, was making her way to high ground as ordered, but Raelyn didn't know how long that would take.

There wasn't a second to spare. Keeping her head down and her rifle wedged up against her shoulder, she ran into the street. "Police! Drop your weapons! Now!"

At least five kids turned to see her heading toward them. Rather than dropping their weapons as ordered, one lifted his gun to fire at her. Thankfully, the bullet went high. She didn't hesitate to return fire, hitting him in the lower abdomen. The force of the bullet finding its mark had him dropping his weapon. She took aim at the next perp, but it seemed as if the reality of the situation had finally hit them because the four remaining kids turned and ran toward the church.

Oh no. She was not going to allow them to use the church as a hiding spot. Not when there were almost a dozen bodies littering the street.

"Four perps possibly armed heading inside the church," she said into her mic as she broke into a run. "One down with a belly wound, he needs a bus." Her step faltered when she reached the young man she'd hit. He was lying on the ground sobbing in pain as he held his hands over the wound in his abdomen.

He didn't look a day older than sixteen.

"Apply pressure," she said, resisting the urge to kneel beside him. "Ambulance will be here soon." It wasn't easy to ignore his pleading eyes, but she didn't dare stop to provide aid. Those kids who'd run inside the church were likely armed, the way everyone in this disaster seemed to be. For all she knew, there were innocent people inside the church.

People that could be used as targets or hostages.

Covering the distance without delay, she swiftly mounted the three steps leading up to the main entrance. Keeping to the side, she drew the door open. Staying back, she listened intently and braced herself for the sound of gunfire.

Hearing nothing, she peeked around the corner. The interior of the church was dimly lit, making it difficult to see clearly. Easing around the doorway, she stepped farther into the church, still holding her weapon ready. She took one step up the center aisle, sweeping her gaze from left to right, then abruptly stopped when she saw one of the four boys who'd come inside holding a mixed-race man dressed in a black shirt and black slacks with a white collar at his throat at gunpoint.

"Stay back!" the kid shouted. "I'll cap him!"

"You don't want to do that," the dark-haired man said calmly. He was young, maybe her own age of thirty, and didn't seem the least bit alarmed. "Killing a man leaves a stain on your soul. God is watching over you."

"Shut up!" the kid shouted, looking nervously from side to side. Was he expecting backup from his friends? "You! Stay where you are, pig!"

Raelyn did as the kid demanded. She forced herself to sound reasonable. "Okay, I won't come any farther. You're the one calling the shots here. What's your name?"

"Drop the gun! Do it! I swear I'll shoot him!" The kid's wild eyes seemed to bore into her. Maybe he was on drugs, which would explain at least part of this debacle.

She didn't want to lower her weapon, but the serene and startling blue eyes of the pastor being held hostage gave her hope that he knew this kid. That even if the punk ran off, they'd be able to track him down later. "Okay. I hear you. I'm lowering my gun, see?" She made an exaggerated movement of pointing her weapon downward and then bending to set it on the floor. "No reason to shoot. Who are you? What's your name?"

"Shut up!" The kid's eyes were wild with fear and false bravado. If it wasn't for the handgun, which appeared to be a Glock, pressed firmly against the pastor's side, she'd have rushed him. The kid clearly hadn't thought this through. Now that he had the pastor as a hostage, he didn't seem to know what to do.

Time for her to help him out. She was the tactical team's second hostage negotiator. "What do you want?" Raelyn kept her voice soft and not threatening. "Money? A ride out of here? Just tell me what you need and I can help you. I'll call my boss, and he'll bring us whatever you want."

"Money! Yeah, I want money!" The kid's eyes brightened. "I want a million dollars."

"I can get you money," she agreed, trying not to roll her eyes. "But you must know I can't get you a million dollars. There isn't a bank out there that has that much cash on hand." Typical teenager who didn't have a clue as to how the world worked. "How about a thousand dollars and a ride?"

The light in the teenager's eyes dimmed. Then suddenly a weariness crossed his features. "Forget it. You can't help me. No one can." The heavy note of despair in the teenager's voice hit like a sucker punch to the gut. He looked as if he'd lost everything. What on earth had happened out on the street? Before she could ask anything more, the kid deliberately turned the barrel of the gun toward her. Gut instinct had her hitting the floor seconds before the weapon reverberated in his hand. A bullet whizzed past her head. She kept moving, scooping the rifle up from the floor and rolling to her knees, bringing the barrel around to return fire.

"No!" The dark-haired man with blue eyes and light-caramel skin abruptly stepped into her line of fire.

"Move it!" She glared at him with annoyance, then jumped to her feet and rushed past him toward the back of the church. But it was too late.

The armed kid was gone.

"WHAT IS WRONG WITH YOU?" The pretty cop whirled on him, anger sparking in her amber eyes. "Why did you let him get away?"

"He's just a kid." Isaiah did his best to remain calm,

although the sound of gunfire had taken him back to the night he'd almost died.

To the night he'd heard his grandmother's voice telling him to go to the light. Followed by God telling him it wasn't his time.

"He fired at a police officer," she snapped. "I don't care if he's a kid, he attempted to shoot a cop. Not to mention holding you hostage and threatening to kill you."

He glanced at the name tag that identified her last name as Lewis. "He was scared. Can you blame him? They were surrounded by cops out there."

"Yeah, I can blame him." Officer Lewis stepped closer, getting right into his face. "He shouldn't have a gun or threaten to kill people. Especially a cop. And I should arrest you for aiding and abetting a criminal."

He nodded sagely. "You could do that. But those charges won't stick. By the way, we haven't met. I'm Pastor Isaiah Washington, and this is my church."

Her eyes widened briefly before narrowing again. "I don't care if you're the pope. I'll toss your butt in jail."

"This isn't a Catholic church. We're nondenominational, so all are welcome." Isaiah spread his hands. "Even you, Officer Lewis."

There was a flash of something he couldn't quite identify in her gaze before she said, "Knock it off already. I want that kid's name. And the names of the others who came inside with him. Right now!"

Isaiah slowly shook his head. "I'm afraid I can't give you that information."

"Can't or won't?" She took another threatening step toward him, her expression grim. "Do you understand how serious this is? There are injured or dead police officers outside, along with other dead civilians, many of them barely old enough to drive. I want the names of those kids who ran through here, or I will place you in handcuffs."

She had no way of knowing that this wouldn't be his first arrest. Granted, it had been ten years since he'd done time in jail. Yet she didn't really understand who he was or the role he played in this community. Over time, he'd become a leader within the city, someone people looked up to for hope. For guidance. For acceptance.

He'd answered God's call. Every day was a gift. One he intended to cherish.

Isaiah held her gaze. "You have every right to arrest me. I can't stop you. But you should know that the new mayor and his entire family all belong to this church, which is a sanctuary for those in need. Even those who may step across the line of the law. Trust me, I understand better than most the seriousness of this incident. The mayor is just as anxious to stop the violence in the city as you are. Hence the recent rejuvenation of this church."

"I highly doubt that the mayor cares more than I do about the violence in the streets," Officer Lewis said in a curt tone. "I'm the one risking my life out there every day. And those cops who were injured didn't ask to be shot and killed by a gang of ruthless kids either."

That was true. He understood the dilemma she faced, he didn't like thinking of the police officers and other innocent people who had lost their lives today. And the ironic part of this entire situation was that he'd made the call to bring the police here in the first place.

A decision that had blown up in his face.

Waves of despair threatened to overwhelm him. It seemed like every time he made a bit of progress, something like this slapped him back down. For months now, he'd been trying to do the right thing. There would be no end to the violent crime until the entire city cracked down on the illegal guns and drugs. He knew that better than most.

And that was exactly why he wouldn't give up. He would not ignore God's calling. After seeing the light, and nearly dying on the street, he'd turned his life around. After getting out of jail, he worked in a drug rehab facility as a peer counselor, then slowly integrated himself as an informal leader into the community. He preached about God's love, peace, and light. This church and his congregation—small as it might be—were important to him. And those kids who'd run through the place were young enough to be saved. Something he knew wouldn't happen if they were tossed into the system.

He held up his arms, placing his wrists together. "Go ahead and arrest me."

He'd assumed she was bluffing, but in a swift move, she'd slapped a pair of silver cuffs around his wrists. "Pastor Isaiah Washington, you're under arrest for aiding and abetting criminals." Her gaze didn't waver as she went on to read him his rights. That, too, brought a flashback to when he'd been lying in a hospital with his ankle cuffed to the bed after undergoing surgery to repair the bullet wound in his chest. He'd been too doped up on pain meds to really appreciate his rights, but then again, it didn't much matter.

When she finished, she added, "Stay here." After gently pushing him toward one of the church pews, she walked away speaking softly into a radio that was little more than an earpiece.

Despite the seriousness of the situation, he couldn't help smiling wryly at his predicament. He didn't think the DA's office would press charges against him, but then again, the insurrection that had taken place outside the church was horrifying in more ways than one. So much death and destruction. For what?

He lifted his gaze to the crucifix on the wall above the modest altar. If he was to spend more time in jail, so be it. He would take whatever punishment the legal system deemed fit. He could only hope and pray that he'd be set free sooner rather than later.

The pretty cop headed outside, no doubt bringing in reinforcements. He wasn't that concerned about being arrested. She was just trying to make a point.

Yet his job was to save lost souls.

A full ten minutes passed before Officer Lewis returned. He rose to his feet to meet her halfway. "I'm ready."

She scowled as if annoyed by his calm attitude. Her job wasn't easy either. And he could acknowledge that it was likely far more dangerous.

"Let's go." She tugged on his arm and drew him through the church and outside. The scene that greeted him nearly sent him to his knees. Several bodies were lying on the ground in pools of blood. So much like the way he had once been.

He froze, unable to move. To take another step. Had he caused this? Was this all his fault?

Lord, help me! Show me Your way!

"Pastor Washington?" Officer Lewis glared at him, her brow furrowed with suspicion. "What's wrong?"

He couldn't conjure the words to explain his role in the death and destruction he faced. He looked down at the ground, then dropped to his knees to pray.

Another crack of gunfire rang out. The pretty cop threw herself on top of him, slamming him facedown onto the steps as the area erupted into chaos.

"More shots fired!" someone shouted.

Stunned, he tried to lift his head, but Officer Lewis continued to hold him down. And that's when he realized that for the second time in his life, someone had just tried to kill him.